DAMN LOVE

DAMN LOVE

JASMINE BEACH-FERRARA

ig
PUBLISHING

BROOKLYN, NEW YORK

Printed in the United Sates of America.
First Paperback Edition
10 9 8 7 6 5 4 3 2 1

Please direct inquiries to:
Ig Publishing, Inc
392 Clinton Avenue
Brooklyn, New York 11238
www.igpub.com

Library of Congress Cataloging-in-Publication Data
Beach-Ferrara, Jasmine.
  [Short stories. Selections]
  Damn love / Jasmine Beach-Ferrara.
    pages cm
Summary: "Set in San Francisco and North Carolina, the linked stories in Damn Love introduce us to a group of characters struggling
with love in all its complicated forms, including a young doctor who
treats heroin addicts, a newly married gay man who tries to reconcile
with his mother after years of estrangement, a trio of physicists caught
in a surprising love triangle, and a soldier who takes secrets with her
to the Iraqi desert. Together, these stories report from the fault lines
of American life, uncertain territory where identity, risk, and desire
comingle, and where resilience is found in even the most flawed efforts
to connect. "-- Provided by publisher.
ISBN 978-1-935439-78-3 (pbk.)
I. Title.
PS3602.E234D36 2013
813'.6--dc23
                                        2013012280

For Meghann

CONTENTS

STAYIN' ALIVE

I get it. Broken hearts mend and in six months I'll see that we were never right for each other anyway. But this middle distance blows. Like the way Emily asked me to meet her for coffee tonight to talk about god knows what. Or the fact that yesterday morning, I saw her and the new girlfriend—a Silicon Valley software tycoon—in the UCSF lobby. It was just after 8:00 and I'd been on call all night, which means I looked like hell and was drinking coffee on a slatted bench, trying to hide from the particularly anxious pack of internal medicine interns I'm supervising this month. One kid, not yet twenty-one because he skipped all of high school, almost killed a patient last week. We call him Danger Mouse now.

Emily and the tycoon emerged from the elevator laughing. I ducked, slid behind the nearest ficus tree and began a close inspection of its leaves. But one of my interns spotted me and began her approach like a heat-seeking missile. This is the one who last week asked for a letter of recommendation and began listing her extra-curriculars as we peed in adjacent stalls. I scowled at her through the ficus leaves until she retreated.

Even I, who have yet to erase her from the #1 position in my speed dial, could see that Emily was happy as she strolled across the lobby, her arm around the tycoon's tubby waist. We were together for seven years—my final year of med school, my residency and the first two years of my infectious disease fellowship. That final year, I probably shouldn't count because it overlapped with the affair. A month ago, she moved out of our apartment on Guerrero and into the tycoon's Castro condo. Now they are everywhere and growing, like a mold. This was the second time I'd seen them in as many weeks. San Francisco is like this: small in precisely the ways you wish it wasn't. Shit-fuck, I call them.

But I can also say this. Last night, I got out of clinic early and picked up a steak burrito on the way home. I crashed on the couch and watched the second half of the Redskins-Cowboys game without having to say a word to anyone. Small triumphs, I know. But they've got to count for something.

Most of my patients are heroin addicts trying, at least some days, to get clean, and gay boys with HIV who do well on cocktails until they don't. One of my patients calls himself Weasel and just cycled out of our inpatient rehab unit for the second time. I discharged him this morning, along with bus vouchers and a quick hug. At the end of appointments, I always hug my patients. Even in San Francisco, this has earned me a bit of a reputation. But in the last year, it also means I've said a proper, final good-bye to six people.

We have Weasel on a new cocktail and on Testosterone, and he's gaining muscle mass like a sixteen-year-old. He calls his biceps guns and flirts with our entire staff, regardless of age and gender. Three months ago, he arrived at the ER with PCP and a T cell count of 15. There is a 90% chanced he will relapse in the next six months. You stay matter of fact about these things until you can't any longer. Which is another way to say that even steady exposure to suffering is no inoculation against it. You see the whole world in a hospital. Emily. Weasel. My interns. The thirty patients I'm following this week. A banquet of souls, my attending likes to say. He means the ghosts too, the ones who die here.

My uncle Roger died on the street a year ago, but he was called at our ER, a fact I discovered only after I identified his body at the city morgue. With Roger, it was always about near misses. That's how it was in 1982, the year that he lived with us. At the time, I thought that he was seventeen, but he was actually twenty-five. I was seven then and all that I cared about was football and convincing people that I was a boy. The Redskins were my team, the closest NFL franchise to our apartment in Durham, North Carolina. For Halloween, I dressed as Joe Theismann and my two best friends, Peter and Keisha, dressed as Hogs, the nickname for the offensive linemen that protected the small quarterback.

Roger looked enough like John Travolta to occasionally persuade drunk women that he was him, in town for a shoot. He usually wore a pair of tight Levi's, a white undershirt, scuffed brown cowboy boots and a denim jacket that smelled of cigarettes and motor oil. His standard expression, in response to praise, scolding, flirtation, and accusations, was a suppressed grin. My infatuation with Roger was mistaken as a crush by my parents, who seemed encouraged that I was showing signs of a burgeoning heterosexuality. But it was something other than that: I wanted to be him. I wanted his efficient, rakish handsomeness to be my own.

I had spotted two tattoos on his body—a blue cross on his forearm that had been inked by an ex-girlfriend and an Apache symbol on his chest, at the spot where you would perform chest compressions. He caught me staring at this one as he passed me in the hall en route to the shower. Towel around his waist, hairbrush as microphone, he was singing "Stayin' Alive." *"Music loud and women warm. I've been kicked around since I was born. And now it's alright, it's ok ..."* My mom was laughing and I was dancing down the hall behind him. Later, he showed me the book he'd found the Apache design in. *It means potency*, he told me seriously. I decided that I would get a tattoo exactly like his, just as I would buy a pocket knife like the one he carried on his belt. The tattoo I eventually got on my hip matches one on Emily's.

Roger slept on the fold-out couch in our apartment. Each morning he folded the couch up and stored his suitcase in the hall closet, leaving no evidence that he lived there. Whenever I was alone in the apartment, I always went straight for his stuff. I'd put on his boots and his aviator sunglasses and pose in front of the mirror nailed to the back of the bathroom door. Standing there, I didn't see a girl with patches on the knees of her jeans and a missing front tooth. I simply saw a body that might grow to be like my uncle's, a body that could get you through the world. It was essential, I knew, that everything be back in place by the time my mom returned with my baby brother strapped to her chest and grocery bags in both arms.

My uncle had already been kicked out of my grandparents' house twice by the time he landed with us. They lived in a southern Ohio town so debilitated by the shutdown of a GoodYear plant that it made downtown Durham, with its abandoned tobacco warehouses and snaking train tracks, feel like a vibrant urban center. Roger was trying to get clean and it was this that he and my mother talked about when they stayed up late chain smoking at the kitchen table.

On those nights, I would crawl across the carpeted floor of my room and nudge the door open as if I was a clever dog. The apartment would be thick with the smells of cigarette smoke and instant coffee. I would poke my head just far enough into the hall to hear her laughter and their conversation. From down the hall, my father's snores rumbled like a diesel engine.

Roger brought out a side of my mom that my father and I couldn't. We were both jealous. With him, she laughed harder than she ever did with us and it was usually impossible to tell what exactly was so funny. A used car ad on TV, my uncle's dead on impression of their mother, the smell of bleach—any of these things could set them off. It sometimes felt as if they were gloating in how much humor there was to be found in the world, if only you knew where to look for it. Even her speaking voice changed with him, a little higher, a little more alive. My father and I tried to console each other with rolled eyes and shrugs, but we both wanted to laugh that hard, and, more than that, longed to make her laugh like that.

Last month, I got home from the hospital and found Emily emptying her desk into a cardboard box. Two packed suitcases were lined up by the front door.

"What's going on?" I poured myself a shot of Jameson. Through the living room window, I glimpsed a car idling outside our building, its headlights like startled, jaundiced eyes.

"I'm moving out," she said. I sunk into the couch.

We'd been fighting and we hadn't seen each other for more than thirty consecutive minutes that week. It's no way to live, and I know that. But we were only months away from a different kind of life, one in which I'd be working fifty instead of eighty hours a week.

She took a deep breath "I've fallen in love with someone else," she said as if announcing that she'd gotten a new job. Emily's currently a bartender, but she's also cut hair, taught first grade, cleaned houses, and done retail. Paid work is largely a distraction from writing confessional, mostly bad poetry. I can say that now although for years I sat gamely in the front row of her packed readings and tried to ignore how closely her poems resembled those of her friends.

"You can't be serious." I stood up and stepped to the door, blocking her way out.

She bent to pick up a suitcase. She'd left before, for a night or two, but never with more than her purse. "C'mon, babe. This is absurd." I tried laughing but she reached for the doorknob. I grabbed her forearm. When she tried to pull away I gripped her wrist more tightly and pulled her towards me.

"Let go of me," she said, her breath warm against my face.

I squeezed until I could feel the speeding beats of her pulse.

"You're hurting me," she said and when I let go, she jerked away as if I was radioactive and in that moment the floor and bookshelves began to shake. Car alarms went off up and down the street. Dishes rattled in the kitchen. When it passed, a radiant look spread across Emily's face. She always hated these minor quakes, which happen every few months out here. But this one she interpreted as a booming geological exclamation point to the utter rightness of her departure. I took it as further evidence that if God exists at all, he is either a twisted bastard or a space cadet.

She walked out and I followed her down the hall and out to the sidewalk, the tycoon joined the scene, ballsy enough to extend her hand for an introduction before she loaded Emily's bags into the trunk. Emily went blank and mute as she got in the passenger's seat, tears rolling down her cheeks as I begged her to stay and the tycoon, behind the wheel by then, put a pale, venous hand on her thigh. For two blocks, I chased them, keeping their tail lights in sight. And then the tycoon gunned it and they were gone. I called Peter sobbing. We've been best friends since we were six and now he and his fiancée, Felix, live a block away. He found me on the sidewalk and I spent the next week with them, calling in sick and vacating my apartment as if it had been condemned.

The year Roger lived with us, my parents were broke and sleep deprived. At their worst, they seemed barely able to tolerate each other. For years, those fights presented like the symptoms of a looming divorce. Now they seem to have been nothing more than the awkward, bucking alignments of one life to another, full of chafe and struggle and moments of ecstatic recognition.

In the winter of 1982, my father's father had a heart attack in Philadelphia. My parents bundled my brother into our battered Corolla and raced to his hospital bed, leaving Roger and me alone for the weekend. I wanted them to stay away for an entire year, during which I would cook dinner for Roger every night and we would somehow get tickets to the SuperBowl, and he, rather than my exhausted parents and wailing brother, would cheer from the sidelines during my Pop Warner football games.

After my game that Saturday, we headed to Duke Forest on his bike. Roger rode helmetless and I wore a beat up football helmet that he'd bought at a yard sale and painted maroon with a gold stripe in honor of the Redskins. I wrapped my arms around his waist and felt tough and terrified as we sped down two-lane back roads. He pushed the bike into the woods and after half a mile on the main trail, we forked off onto a minor dirt path that ran along the Eno River.

Other than the tall, swaying pines, the trees were bare. Dry, fallen branches cracked under our feet and ice pocked the trail. Behind him, I tried to imitate his swagger. When he accidentally stepped in a puddle, I followed suit. The frigid water soaked through my sneakers and socks. By the time we stopped to rest at a bend in the river, my toes were numb.

"It's easy," he said, continuing his primer on cussing. "Just pretend you're saying a normal word. Like this. Money. Toast. Dog. Fuck." We were squatting on the bank next to the river, the soles of our shoes gripping the sticky red mud. He rolled a joint and I scanned the shallows of the river's clear water for skipping stones. I had never cussed before. He licked the rolling paper with his tongue, a quick flash of pink, and then lit up.

"Let's start with shit. That's an easier one," he said. "You've heard your parents saying that, right?"

I nodded.

"It's ok," he said. "I'm the only one who can hear you."

I dipped my hand into the water and selected a chipped, misshapen stone. I hurled it into the dark water in the middle of the river where it immediately sunk. "Shit," I ventured. My hand was now as cold as my feet and it occurred to me that perhaps there were ways to impress him that didn't involve being so uncomfortable.

"Excellent," he smiled, palming the crown of my head with his hand and squeezing it. Blood surged to my heart. Year later, I would take Peter to this spot during the six months that we dated during our senior year of high school. We would sit by the river and make out, both of us eager for the distraction of conversation. A few times, I tried to explain what it had been like to be there with Roger, but then, as now, it was hard to get it right.

That day in 1982, it took another hour for Roger and me to circle back to the trail head. As we walked, I watched the brown and whites of the river rushing by, the barn-red flare of a cardinal swooping through the trees, Roger's shoulder bent and his palm cupped around the joint to shield it from the breeze. I stayed close enough to make sure that he could hear me whispering fuck to the sparrows hopping from branch to branch and asshole to the low-hanging pine boughs that brushed my cheeks.

The next night, we watched the Redskins play the Eagles. Roger had heated up two TV dinners and I tried to coax myself into an appetite for Salisbury steak. "Do you think they'll make the Super Bowl," I asked, soaking a chunk of gristly meat in steaming brown gravy.

"Highly likely," he replied, tearing the plastic sheath off his cherry pie.

"We could have a party," I suggested.

"That's a long time from now," he said.

"It's the same day as my birthday."

"I know," he said and for several minutes we watched the game in silence, as Darryl Green picked off a pass and, three plays later, Theismann connected with the lanky Art Monk on a twenty-five yard slant into the end zone. After the extra point, the Redskins were down by two with five minutes to play. During the commercial break, Roger pulled his jackknife out of the leather pouch on his belt. The knife had a single gleaming blade and a wooden handle with brass tips. "Give me your thumb," he said as he drew the blade quickly across his own thumb and then squeezed until a drop of blood appeared.

"You'll barely feel this," he said, looking directly at me and smiling. I was scared but calm, the same feeling I would have years later when I kissed Keisha for the first time. He angled the tip of the knife into the pad of my thumb. The cut was no bigger than a pin prick. He pushed his thumb against mine and explained that we were now blood brothers, which meant that no matter what happened, we were bound to one another.

For the rest of game we held hands and when, in the final minute, John Riggins chugged his way across the goal line to put the Redskins up by four, we both jumped up and screamed, arms raised and whooping. As the clock ran down, my uncle stood in front of the TV doing the Hog dance, and I thought, as I had the day before at the river, that we would go on and on like this.

It's hard, when thinking of Roger, to isolate one image from another. The problem is that these images do not add up to a whole. They are partial. Like him, it is tempting to say. But that wouldn't be quite right. He was as whole any of us, but he worshipped his own gods. More times than I can count, I've been asked why I went into medicine. By admissions committees, professors, now students. Each time, it's Roger's face—a young grinning heartbreaker a moment away from trouble—that comes to mind. But that's never the answer I give.

God forbid you bleed a little, Emily would say. She thinks I live in a bubble because I go to cocktail parties at which someone is invariably talking about his wine collection and someone else is casually relating how she met the Obamas. Emily hated these parties as much as she hated the fact that I sometimes like them. More and more often, we would arrive late and depart early to hang out at the bar where she works.

When she left, Peter suggested that I get a pet. A companion animal, he means. With her gone, my apartment is as blank as a hotel suite. Emily somehow took the charm with her. Now the salvaged chair in the living room exudes a whiff of wreckage rather than warmth. The bookcase she painted pink has lost its whimsy and looks like it belongs at a Head Start. The thriving plants and the sunlight streaming through open windows and her photos clustered on the walls—that was all her.

She left home and Alabama at sixteen. The great escape, she calls it. From there, she worked her way west. The word *hope* is tattooed on the inside of her forearm. She got it in rehab. Several of her friends have the same tattoo. *Just talk to me*, she would say, coming up behind me while I worked at my desk, her arms around my chest, her hand on my heart. I wouldn't look up. *We're all gonna die*, Alex, *no matter how many journal articles you read tonight. Come to bed*, she'd say, naked and tangled in our sheets. Or, later, *come out with me*, her jeans tight, her lipstick fresh. That I kept studying was a problem.

The one photo she left behind is of Peter. In it, he's standing outside his parents' brick rancher in Durham. He's wearing a gray t-shirt and his eyes are staring straight at the camera. She took it at three in the morning when the moon was nearly full. Somehow she got the lighting on his face right. Looking at it feels like being with him. Behind him, the lawn was meticulously cut, his father's handiwork. The house was dark and shuttered except for the porch light, its glow competing with the moon's in the photo.

It was the night of my med school graduation from Carolina. She and Peter had flown in together from San Francisco; late that night, after dinner with my family and then drinks at a bar, Peter had asked if we could drive by his parents' house. He hadn't been home since his dad kicked him out back when we were in college. Emily was the one who suggested he actually get out of the car. She snapped thirty, forty shots, her voice soft as she coaxed him from the edge of the lawn to the front stoop. That was six years ago now.

The week she moved out, I lived with Peter and Felix. From their guest room, I could see my building's front door. I spent more hours than I care to confess watching for signs of Emily's return. I also logged into her email and read the horribly love-drenched messages she and the tycoon were exchanging. I got as far as writing a message to the tycoon from Emily's account cancelling a weekend trip to Sonoma. When I called Peter asking him to edit it for believability he ordered me to turn the computer off. *I'll be home in an hour*, he said.

I was high that week. Which meant that when I wasn't stalking Emily, I was eating Fritos and chocolate icing by the spoonful. I don't have an addictive personality, so I can get high twice a year or every morning and it makes no real difference. People like to put addicts in a separate category, on the other side of a bridge so long you cannot see its end. But, more than anything, the patients I see feel familiar to me. I don't need to know why Weasel has relapsed six times, or why another patient, an oncologist who has been positive for ten years and has an undetectable viral load, spent last weekend on a meth-fueled binge on a gay cruise. I differ with the twelve-step orthodoxy on this point. I don't believe these things require exhaustive explanation. They are simply the risks we each choose, not so different really than boarding a plane or deciding to live on the West Coast.

More and more, I hear people talking about *the big one* as if they can somehow stop it. Even Peter and Felix have a survival kit. Assembling it was on their wedding planning to–do list, a state of preparedness somehow linked to matrimony. From deep in the bowels of FEMA's website, they downloaded an Earthquake Survival Guide, which promises to keep you safe for the first thirty-six hours. That's how long they think it will take to get aid into the city. This coming from the geniuses who didn't even know there were people in the Superdome.

So now a plastic garbage can on wheels sits in their backyard, filled with glow sticks, canned food, blankets, cash, a first aid kit, and gallons of water. I can't imagine pushing that thing through the busted streets of an apocalyptic San Francisco and trying to outrace death. If the earth splits open at these coordinates, I will either fall through or stand on the rim and administer first aid.

Emily. Weasel. Roger. Peter. Felix. Love. Death. Risk. All these pieces fit. My seeing Emily yesterday morning means nothing more than that we are still in each other's orbits. But it also distracted me enough that I missed a patient's allergy to an antibiotic and prescribed it to her. Danger Mouse caught my mistake. Near misses are what I'm talking about here.

On January 30, 1983, I turned eight, and the Redskins kicked off against Miami in the SuperBowl. Although it was a school night, my parents let me throw a party. I invited Peter and Keisha and requested that they each dress as a Redskin. We made an unlikely trio—me, a female Joe Theismann, Peter a faggy, reluctant Art Monk, and, in Keisha, a Darrell Green with braids.

We spent the pre-game show assembling a SuperBowl shrine out of my Legos and Redskins curios. Its centerpiece was a battery-operated talking Redskins helmet. Peter was bored out of his skull but perked up slightly when he saw the cheerleaders' routine. We watched the game in near silence on our thirteen-inch black and white Zenith, its rabbit ears wrapped in foil. My father sat in his recliner, working on a beer and trying to stay awake. Every few minutes my mother, who hated football, cheerily inquired if anyone had scored. My brother was asleep in the room we shared.

When Theismann scrambled on a third and ten and slid for a first down during the second quarter, I thought of Roger, and how, had he been there, we would have high-fived. Minutes later, when the Dolphins cruised into the lead with a seventy-six yard touchdown pass, I muttered "Shit." On either side of me, Peter and Keisha giggled but my parents failed to react. "Fuck," I said, this time more loudly.

"Watch it, young lady," my father said, raising his eyebrows. I scowled at him.

He'd kicked Roger out of our apartment. Twice that week, I had found my mother crying at the kitchen table and the night before the SuperBowl, she and my father had fought again as they'd baked my birthday cake. My mother wanted to give my uncle one more chance; absolutely not, my father had said. But it still seemed possible that Roger would show up at half-time, just as it seemed possible that the Redskins would score twice and hold the Dolphins scoreless for the rest of the game.

Going into the fourth quarter, the Redskins were down 17-13, and for the first time, it occurred to me that they might lose. Keisha and I were gripping each other's hands and Peter, still a star Sunday school pupil at that point, was praying. With just over ten minutes left, the Redskins went for it on a fourth and one. Riggins broke free of a tackle and ran for a forty-three yard touchdown. The clock ticked mercilessly. With 1:55 on the clock, Theismann connected with Charlie Brown in the end zone and my friends and I jumped up and did the Hog dance. Even my father, jolted out of his nap by our screams, joined in. My mother stood behind the couch and took pictures of us with the Polaroid they'd given me at dinner.

The phone rang. I knew that it was Roger even before my mother's voice jumped. The game clock ran down. I watched my mother make eye contact with my father across the room and saw him nod slightly. She signaled for me to come to the phone. I did but I didn't want to talk to Roger.

He was calling from a bar in Reno, he explained, saying that he'd thought about me the whole game. In the background, I could hear music and a woman calling his name and laughing loudly. We talked for a few minutes, but mostly it was him rehashing the highlights with forced enthusiasm. Across the room, I could see Theismann being interviewed, sweat pouring down his face, a sparkling white SuperBowl Champions cap sitting jauntily on his head. I passed the phone back to my mother and ran back into the living room, sliding into position on the couch.

The next time I saw Roger was Christmas Eve of 1990, when he arrived in a taxi and rang our doorbell like a stranger. It took a second to recognize him. His black hair had turned gray, like my mother's, and it was well cut. For the first time, I noticed that his left ear stuck out. There were other changes:

twenty pounds and a two-inch scar under his right eye. He wore a gray wool overcoat and lined black leather gloves. He carried a caramel-colored leather duffel and a slim silver briefcase.

I was seventeen then and had just been accepted into Yale. My parents couldn't afford the tuition and fought about it frequently, my mother arguing for them to re-mortgage the house, my father insisting I stay in state. I was preoccupied by this and by the pressing, and somehow not contradictory, questions of whether to have sex with Peter and whether to tell Keisha that I was in love with her.

Roger and I stood in the living room, crowded by piles of presents and a tree weighed down by handmade ornaments. We fell into an easy conversation. That night, he and my mother stayed up late at the kitchen table. She and I got up early the next morning and took a bottle of aftershave from my father's stack of gifts and a pack of wool socks from my brother's, readdressing the cards to Roger. My mother raced around the kitchen pulling together a gift basket from the contents of our pantry—an old, unopened bottle of maple syrup, a can of smoked almonds, a box of Darjeeling tea. *What the hell is he going to do with maple syrup?* she muttered. But she couldn't help herself and so arranged and then rearranged these items in a wicker basket she'd found in the basement.

That night, Roger and I smoked up in my backyard. I pretended I'd done it before, but when I started to hack, he handed me his beer and said, *easy there*. He leaned back on his heels and closed his eyes, his head bowed as if he was praying. Behind us, my parents' house glowed and to the north Durham's smokestacks and sedate skyline were visible. Standing next to him in the quiet yard, I felt like an adult. He told me about meeting a CIA spook in Panama, about flying first class and sitting next to Joe Thiesmann on a flight to LA. *He was wearing his SuperBowl ring and a gold bracelet,* he said, shaking his head. W*hatever else you do, promise me you'll stay away from dudes who wear jewelry,* he said. That was the last conversation we ever had.

When my mom leaned out the kitchen door to call us in for dinner, she smelled the pot. I was exiled to my room and then grounded for two weeks. Roger called a cab before my parents could tell him to leave. A month later he was arrested in a federal bust and sentenced to prison in Morganton, a few hours west of Durham. My mother visited him on the third Saturday of each month as if they had a custody agreement. She brought him books from the ten page reading list he'd typed out for her. He liked Hemingway, Cheever, Denis Johnson, John Grisham. It was in prison that he converted, the preferred term now for testing positive, as if someone has become a believer rather than a carrier.

Not until my graduation from medical school did my mother tell me that the contents of that silver briefcase—and not a second mortgage—had paid for my first two years of college. They'd paid taxes on it, she insisted. The details were fuzzy.

We are like most families I know, which means that we're scattered now. My parents, just a year away from retiring, have already purchased the RV that they plan to tour the country in. My brother is married and has a two-year old son. They live in a condo in the Atlanta suburbs, close to his wife's family. He works for a landscaping company and, once a month, djs at a downtown bar. We talk every few weeks and they're coming to visit next month. This is not the life I would have imagined for him, which is different than saying it is not the life that I wanted for him. For years, I confused the two, as if these conditions were indistinguishable.

Roger has been dead for a year now. He overdosed near the Panhandle in Golden Gate Park. He easily could have been one of my patients, but I didn't know he was in the city until my mother called with the news of his death. Emily was out of town and I took a cab from the hospital to the city morgue. An intern escorted me to the viewing room.

He was wrapped in a white sheet and laid out on a steel table. I pulled the sheet down, trying to see his body not as a patient's but as my own flesh and blood. My mother's jaw line. My grandfather's nose. The track marks. Dirt under his nails. The tattoos—the two I'd seen as a child, and another one low on his hip, of a heart, the name Angela in loopy cursive running across it. I nodded and was escorted back out.

By then, he'd been out jail for a few years. Between the time of his release and his death, he was an erratic, fleeting ghost. A year would go by without a call and then he'd be at my parents' doorstep, either flush or broke, sober or high, healthy or off his meds. *You never know which Roger is going to show up*, my mother would say in lieu of actually describing her broken heart.

I flew with his body back to North Carolina two days later. Emily wanted to go with me, but I told her she didn't need to. I meant it and I didn't. Later, she told me this was the first weekend she spent with the tycoon. My parents got security passes so they could meet me at the gate at Raleigh/Durham. The three of us stood at the window and watched the baggage handlers unload his coffin from the rear of the plane as if it was any other kind of freight. We buried him at a cemetery in Durham. My parents bought their own plots there years ago and insisted on showing them to my brother and me that day, weirdly proud of themselves for such clear-sighted acceptance of their own mortality.

Keisha came to the funeral and afterward, she and I had drinks at new bar in downtown Durham. We talked about her husband and about Emily and she told me that she'd recently enlisted in the National Guard. When she said she was ready to go to Iraq if she got called up, I recognized the look in her eyes as the same one I'd seen on her wedding day. She drove me back to my parent's house like we were eighteen again, and we sat in her darkened car for a few minutes with the radio on. When she reached for me, I kissed her and for twenty seconds it was as if we were catapulted into a parallel universe in which all the things that keep us apart didn't matter. Then I pulled back and got out of the car.

This afternoon, I hauled ass to leave the hospital early so I could get home to change and shower before meeting Emily. It meant unloading a few patients on the interns and rushing through their evaluations. Danger Mouse, who yesterday called me a prick when he thought I was out of earshot, got a deserved *poor*.

She'd asked me to meet her at a new café on Valencia, a place where we had no history. It was nearly empty when I arrived. Emily showed up ten minutes late, wearing skinny jeans with a white tank and a white leather belt. Her hair was pulled back and she had on fire engine red lipstick. She ordered a decaf coffee, sat across from me and tapped her index finger on the wooden table. Her fingernails were bitten to the quick.

"You look skinny," she said. "Are you eating?"

I figured I had exactly one chance. "Look, Emily—"

"Have you noticed how Obama always says *look* when he's about to get all, like, didactic. Don't you love Michelle's arms? She's so jacked." She laughed nervously and then looked at her phone to check the time. One minute had elapsed and already her massive chatter shield was up.

"I miss you," I said, my hands flat on the table. I heard somewhere that this is a vulnerable position because it signals that you're not about to pull a .38 from an ankle holster.

Emily looked away. Her mom walked out on her family when she was four and she'd told me early on that it had made her terribly loyal. *I never leave*, she'd whispered. We were lying in the grass at Dolores Park. She was on top of me, kissing my neck.

"I need you," I said and this got her attention. *Are you sure you're not somewhere on the autism spectrum?* she would ask sometimes. *Asperger's maybe?* In the weeks before boards, I'd spend my days off studying for sixteen hours. I'm doing this for us, I'd tell her as I ate dinner at my desk. *What about right now, Alex?* she'd say. *This is us too.*

"I have to tell you something." She paused. A sip of coffee.

"I'm pregnant," she continued. "We're seeing an OB at UCSF and I wanted you to hear it from me first."

"How far along are you?"

"Almost four months."

I barked out a laugh. She left a month ago. For a woman.

"We found, like, the perfect donor and everyone says it takes at least a year. This is like a one in a million thing. But I'm 34, and -"

"I know you're 34."

"I know you know," she said. She'd wanted to get pregnant two years ago. I'd worn her down arguing that we should wait.

She looked me in the eye and it was too much. My throat tightened. Sadness pummeled me. I stared at the table and counted to three in German. It's the trick I use to keep myself from crying when notifying family members of a death. But she knows me.

"Hey," she said, her voice softening for the first time. She touched my wrist with her index finger and left it there.

"Dr. C!"

I glanced up and saw Weasel, my patient, approaching our table. Since leaving the hospital yesterday, he'd shaved his head and started growing a goatee. He grinned and slapped me on the back.

"You're looking good, Weasel," I said. Emily told me that the first seventy-two hours out of rehab were the hardest to get through. But I've also had patients tell me exactly the opposite, that the longer you're on the street, the harder it gets. Either way, right now Weasel is like a man on a razor thin wire, one foot raised, the other wobbling, his arms extended, no net to speak of. Sport for the dead, he once called shooting up as I took his blood pressure and we both stared at his track marks. Then he laughed.

"This one saved my life," he told Emily. "They were about to put me in a hospice and she says, *Weasel, I hear you used to be a boxer.* I guess it's in my chart somewhere. She goes, *I need you to be a fighter.* She believed in me."

For a second, he teared up. He shrugged and blinked them away. Grinning, he flexed his biceps, which rose like firm breasts, filling out his t-shirt sleeves. "Now look at me," he said.

Emily laughed and gave him that NA murmur that's like an amen and they shared a moment. But then she remembered that Weasel was on my team. She checked her phone again. He looked at me, eyebrows cocked. He knows a little about the humiliations of love and seemed to recognize this for what it was. "Don't let me interrupt you, ladies," he said, stepping back, licking his chapped lips.

At the counter, he ordered a cup of coffee and deliberated over the baked goods. *Get some protein, buddy,* I sent him a mental signal. But he went with the bear claw. He bit into the fat, flakey pastry and took a sip of scalding coffee. He looked happy, as if nothing was more real than the sugar dissolving on his tongue.

Emily finished her coffee. "Your patients adore you," she said.

"He's just glad to be alive."

She sighed, as if I had understood nothing. "I have to go. I just needed to tell you in person. I didn't want you hearing it from someone else."

"Jesus, Emily." I reached for her hand and she didn't pull back. I pushed my thumb softly into her palm, the way I had for years. I could feel Weasel's eyes on us but I didn't look up.

"C'mon, Alex," she said softly. "Don't act like this is black and white. I know you're sad but it's not exactly like I broke your heart. You've been in love with Keisha since you were sixteen. Everyone else has been a subletter." She kissed my fingers and extracted her hand.

She stood up. "You'll be fine." She walked out, phone already to her ear.

I ordered a refill. I'm due at Peter's for dinner in an hour, but for the first time in weeks, I have nowhere to be. Four months means the baby is covered with lanugo and can blink and suck his thumb. He is learning how to breathe. I imagined a five-inch fetus inside of her, his withered face set with determination as he winds up for his first kick.

I used to imagine it all the time. A baby with a plume of dark hair swaddled against Emily's chest, my providing for them, us rounding the long bend of our life together. That image of her and the baby is apparently pretty accurate; it's the rest I got wrong. Near misses.

When my father kicked Roger out of our apartment in 1983, I blamed myself. A week before the SuperBowl, I'd had an hour alone in the apartment and I had gone immediately for Roger's cowboy boots. I slid one on, and then, standing up, jammed my foot into the other. Something impaled my heel and I screamed in pain, unable to put my foot down or to shake the boot off.

I heard my mom on the stairs. I was terrified that she would find me in his clothes, so I hid, hopping on one foot into my bedroom and crawling under my bed, squeezing between a box of baby clothes my brother had outgrown and a broken record player that my father kept vowing to fix.

My mother found me covered in dust balls and sweat. Down on her knees, one hand cupping my brother's bald head, she coaxed me out. Her eyes landed on the boots and her eyebrows shot up. It stung, but did not hurt exactly, as she tugged and then twisted until my foot came loose from the boot.

She hissed and sucked in her cheeks, her eyes suddenly frantic. "It's ok, baby," she said to me, her voice gentler than it had been in a long time. I could tell she was trying not to cry as she extracted a syringe from my heel and then wiped away the thin stream of blood trickling down my foot.

When I reached for the needle, my mother swatted my hand away. She was electric with panic. The term AIDS had existed for exactly four months at that point. I'd heard her talking to Roger about it late at night, her tone urgent. She wanted him to get tested and he laughed it off.

From the living room, we heard the front door opening and Roger's singing. The door clicked shut. "Stay here," my mother instructed. My brother began to cry, and without warning, I did too. I was in over my head, sinking in brackish water. I closed my eyes and held my breath. I'd betrayed his secret and mine. I couldn't stand the thought of facing him, but I couldn't resist it either. I crawled to the bedroom door and watched.

He stopped singing as soon as he saw her, charging towards him with the needle like it was a tiny spear. My brother still strapped to her chest, she threw herself at him and pounded his chest until he finally got hold of her wrists. Her cheeks reddened as she screamed. It was about him, about me, about all that she had dared to wish for—an adored little brother who'd stay clean, a little girl who actually wanted to be one—exploding in front of her. He didn't protest or try to explain. He waited until she was done and then he wrapped his arms around her. After that, the apartment became very, very still until my father got home a few hours later. By then, Roger had already packed. But there was still another colossal fight, one that left my mother, brother and me crying, my uncle escaping into the night and my father sweating with rage.

Before leaving the next morning, my uncle took me on a short walk around the parking lot and explained that he needed to move on, that there was a job waiting for him at a bar in Reno. I nodded seriously and tried to calculate how much money I would need to save in order to visit him.

With him gone, the apartment was desperately quiet. It felt empty rather than crammed. Each time I walked into the living room, I expected to see his boots lined neatly against the wall and his jacket on the folding chair next to the door. Every time that I found them once again not there, it was like missing a step as you walk downstairs, that slight lurch in your stomach, that teetering before you regain your balance.

Last year, Roger knew I was in San Francisco, but he never contacted me. And I never saw him at the mobile clinic. Once a week, I go out with the van and we do the rounds—Church and Market, the Tenderloin, the Panhandle, a few stops in Golden Gate Park. I was in his territory. I saw and treated countless men like him, men like Weasel. By then, he may have been so far gone that he wouldn't have taken any help. I think about it though. If he'd stepped up into the van, could have we saved him? It would have meant another round of rehab and finding the right cocktail. It would have meant another long road.

Despite myself, there are times when I think I see him in a crowd. Walking down Mission on my way to get a burrito. A flash of his face through the window of a BART train pulling out of the station. I see him as a lost, charming young man. Or as he would be now, heavier, darkened by the world, but still striving for something beyond the measure allotted him.

Sometimes, this happens with patients too. The ones I thought could make it to old age, or at least to their next check up. The ones whose deaths I was least prepared for. That's why at the end of every appointment I say good-bye and hug them. They get used to it and sometimes it's a side hug, so quick they barely notice. These are habits, gestures, as much as they are small, urgent blessings.

These are the things we do. The way, out here, we have built an entire city atop the San Andreas Fault, as if it really could sustain all this weight, all this life.

Emily's gone and pregnant. Peter's getting married. Keisha still hasn't been sent to Iraq. Weasel's back from the dead and grinning. I saw Roger's body.

I know he's dead. I get it.

But there are still moments when he's right here with me, when it's like we're back in those woods again and I'm racing to keep up. In a second, he'll slow down long enough to turn around and flash that damned grin of his. Then he's off again, running a slant pattern, brushing past trees as if they were linebackers, arms outstretched, eyes locked on the ball.

These aren't the kind of things we speak of often. But the dead, I have found, are strangely loyal companions. They leave, but they also come back, the way, I know, Emily will not. It's as if they cannot stay away, as if—even more than us—they cannot bear the grief.

DIFFERENT PATHS, SAME WOODS

For six months, the invitation to her son's wedding sat in Ruth's underwear drawer like a love letter, tucked behind a mound of folded pastel cottons and the one lace thong she owned. The sleek gray envelope was addressed only to her. *Ruth Fearrington* it read in black calligraphy, as if Ronny didn't even exist. She hadn't told Ronny about it, and she wouldn't. If anything was going to convince him to reconcile with their son, it was not Peter's wedding to another man.

Now that the day had arrived, she knew she'd made the right choice. Aside from the obvious, she had finished another round of chemo and was coming off four days with her face in the toilet, grateful for the tiniest things—the symmetrical, gleaming tiles under her knees, the soft, cool washcloth Ronny placed on her neck, a thirty-minute reprieve between retching.

But this morning, she'd held down a cup of hot tea and a piece of unbuttered toast. She was sitting on the rear deck in jeans and a t-shirt and the morning sun was shining on her face and her bald head, slathered with 70 sunscreen. At home, she didn't bother with the wig unless she and Ronny were entertaining or making love.

He had finished the laundry and paid the bills, so she had nothing to do today except soak up the sun and go to brunch and a matinee with her best friend, Janet. Their sweet, dopey hound, Buster, was asleep at her feet, too old and arthritic now to join Ronny on his Saturday hunting trips.

It was the first week of deer season and by now, he would be deep in the woods of southern Orange County. He'd retired from his job as a US History teacher a year earlier and worked part-time time in kitchens and plumbing at the new Home Depot near SouthPointe Mall. The moon had still been shining when he'd gotten up that morning, extracting himself from her arms and dressing in the dark, packing his truck with a cooler, a pair of camo coveralls, and the ridiculous orange vest he wore so he didn't get his head shot off. But it could be worse, she knew. Janet's sister's husband had recently announced that he was in love with his thirty-two year old trainer at their gym.

The deck was a birthday gift from Ronny. Like all of his projects, it was beautifully executed, the cherry stain gleaming, the nails evenly sunk, a discreet nook for his gas grill. They'd lived in the three-bedroom ranch since 1974, the year that Peter was born and that Ronny returned home to Durham from his final tour. After Peter went to college, they'd added the den. Later, when it became clear he wouldn't be visiting, they'd turned Peter's room into a craft studio where she made ornaments for their church's annual Christmas fundraiser.

More recently, Ronny had redone the kitchen and both bathrooms. Nothing could be done about the house's boxy, brick exterior, but with each addition, its interior more closely resembled the home Ruth wished they could afford. She was proud of what they'd done with it. The neighborhood kept changing, though. A tienda had opened up a block from them, its front windows plastered with ads for phone cards that she couldn't read and the bright jerseys of Mexican soccer teams. There was now a halfway house for ex-cons a few streets over, and Ronny taught weekly Bible Study there with a friend from his North Baptist's Men's Group. Their new neighbor on the right was an artist who refused to mow her law or to let Ronny do it for her.

To be polite, they had gone to an opening of hers at a down-town gallery a few months ago, but all her paintings had been nude self-portraits. Ronny could barely make eye contact with her after that. The paintings weren't even that good; her face looked flat and she'd clearly been blindfolded when she'd done her boobs and hips.

Thinking of all this made Ruth laugh. Cancer did that, at least: helped sift the essential from the mundane. The sun was warm on her skin and that was real, as was the smooth half-acre of grass that stretched out behind the house. She loved walk-ing barefoot through the grass to pick corn, tomatoes and ber-ries from Ronny's garden. And they were just a few miles away from Duke Forest where for decades she'd hiked the trails. Those woods were one of the great joys of her life. In them, she felt most like the girl she'd once been, the one who'd collected bugs and who'd wanted, until she'd barely passed chemistry junior year, to be a scientist.

Her cell phone rang. Buster barked once and then fell back into his nap. She answered, expecting to hear Janet's voice.

"Mrs. Davis?" a man asked.

"Speaking," Ruth said, slipping into the smooth, vacant tone she used to take calls at the pediatrician's office where she worked as a receptionist.

"This is Felix Rivera."

She hesitated, unable to place his name.

"Peter's Felix."

"Oh," she said.

"I know this is unexpected, so let me get right to the point. There's a ticket waiting for you on a 12:05 non-stop flight today out of Raleigh-Durham. It arrives four hours before the cer-emony and a driver will take you directly to the hotel. I booked a room for you and a return flight for Monday." His voice was smooth and deep, unlike Peter's, which bore a lilt that some-times made her cringe.

Ruth didn't know what to say, so she went with good man-ners. "That's certainly generous," she began. "But I don't see how it would be possible." When she'd asked Dr. Patel about flying, he'd frowned and pushed his rimless glasses up on his nose. He'd gotten her this far—through the breast cancer eight years ago and now this run in with lymphoma—and she trusted him with her life. The chocolate cakes she baked for him and his new wife before each visit were the best way she knew to say this. Last fall, when one of her scans had come up clear, Ronny had delivered a cooler full of frozen venison steaks and sausage to Dr. Patel's house, surprising the doctor in the midst of a dinner party.

"At least take the flight information," Felix persisted. She'd never met him and knew only that he was a lawyer and that his parents would be at the wedding.

She jotted the flight number down on the border of the crossword puzzle she was doing in the *News & Observer*, and then hung up and closed her eyes. She longed to see Peter and she understood the clear overture he'd made by inviting her. But he wanted her there only under the condition that she be genu-inely happy for him. That would never happen and she couldn't pretend otherwise. The kindest thing she could do was stay home and keep her mouth shut. It was all too much to think about. The inevitable fight. Her health. Ronny's reaction.

Months earlier, she'd gotten as far as checking ticket prices and visiting the website of the hotel where the ceremony would take place and where out-of-town guests were encouraged to stay. But the rates at the W Hotel were more than the monthly payment on Ronny's new truck. The Hampton Inn in Ashe-ville, where they vacationed each August, was more her style. Although she hadn't seen Peter in almost thirteen years she could tell, from his tone in their conversations, from the wedding invitation, that he'd become a snob.

There was a man at their church who used to be that way. The Sunday after Easter, he'd given a testimonial and had called his fiancée up to the altar, where they stood hand in hand. "We're all sinners," he had said through his tears. "And the great miracle is that Jesus loves us anyway." She thought that if Peter could just hear this story, it might move him the way it had her.

Janet knew all about it and had been urging her to go. *I know I'm not a mother*, Janet would say, choosing her words carefully, *but it seems like all he wants is to know you love him.* Ruth had confided in no one else. Who would she tell? Her mother thought it was 1963 and cried about JFK's assassination every night over another nursing home dinner of canned green beans, boiled chicken and cherry jello. She had her Women's Group at North Baptist, and the girls at work, but it wasn't the kind of subject you bring up casually.

Peter didn't know she was sick and she preferred it that way. She didn't want him visiting out of guilt or pity. He needed to choose to return home. He hadn't set foot in the house since the Christmas of his junior year of college. They'd gotten back from the Christmas Eve service and were about to open presents when Peter made his announcement. They were sitting in front of the fire, eggnog poured, Bing Crosby playing, wrapped presents spilling out from under the tree. *Don't ever come back here*, Ronny had spat out, and thirty minutes later Peter was slipping into the passenger seat of Alex's idling car. As they'd pulled away, Ruth had realized that Alex—Peter's best friend since childhood and high school girlfriend—had been waiting for Peter's call, that it had all been staged in a sense. She had imagined Alex's family taking him in like a wounded stray. She had been humiliated and bereft. How could she have known that both father and son would act like those stupid words uttered by Ronny were a blood oath? She didn't like it anymore than Ronny did, but she held onto a hope that Peter would change. Once, she'd found Ronny thumbing through baby pictures of Peter in the garage, his eyes dark. But he refused to talk about their son, and until recently, she'd felt that she couldn't go behind his back.

Over the years, she'd followed Peter's career online, reading his articles in the *San Francisco Chronicle* and in the magazines he freelanced for. They'd been back in touch for two years now, after she'd emailed him in response to a birthday card he'd sent. It was a compromise position, one that she'd consulted with her pastor over. He had given his blessing and this mattered to her.

When she'd last seen him at age twenty, Peter had looked just like Ronny. They had the same lanky body and square jaw, the same slow grin. There was a picture of Peter and Felix on the wedding invitation, standing on an empty Pacific beach. Peter had filled out and his hair brushed his collar. His eyebrows looked waxed and his body leaned easily into Felix's. They were both dressed in white linen pants and collared shirts.

In one of their calls, she'd asked him if he ever wore dresses. "Yes," he'd said after a pause. "But it doesn't mean I want to be a woman."

"I've never known it to mean anything else," she had replied.

"It's about performance," Peter had shot back and she had let it stop there.

It was late—she usually called him after Ronny went to bed—and she had been sipping a glass of chardonnay in the family room, the lights off, the moon casting a bright beam onto the wooden floor. In the dark, she felt like she could say anything to him. She asked questions and in response, he often surprised her with his candor. He rarely had questions for her though, and she couldn't quite explain why she held her tongue when it came to describing her life. She would murmur vaguely in response to Peter's various, odd confessions: the affairs that weren't really affairs because no one objected; the possibility that he and Felix would somehow have a child.

They maneuvered through these calls as if they were dismantling a bomb. One wrong move and it would be over. But she pushed on. She had to. Nothing could be worse than his absence, as pure and aching a wound as she'd known.

Later, she had tried to imagine him in a dress, something black and more expensive than anything she owned. She could see the padded bra, his hips canted, a sly satisfaction on his face. It bothered her that he insisted on calling it performance. Over the years, the pediatrician she worked for had seen a handful of kids with this problem, and it inevitably led to a diagnosis and a referral to a psychiatrist. You could always spot them in the waiting room, boys with big delicate eyes and movements like a young deer's, girls with round little biceps and wide stances. And quiet, always quiet, sticking close to their parents as the other kids played in the waiting room.

A few times, she had found Peter in her negligees and heels when he was a boy. It had scared her. Those first few years of school, he'd come home crying on a handful of afternoons. How do you tell your six-year-old boy he's going to get himself killed if he doesn't watch it? But he'd figured this out on his own and by the time he was eight or nine, he had asked to join Alex's Pop Warner football team, and soon enough he had become a bookish teenager and joined the school newspaper. She had breathed a sigh of relief as she helped him with his boutonniere the night of Senior Prom. When he left to pick up Alex, he had seemed genuinely happy and she'd felt like she'd done a major part of her work as his mother. The next morning, she'd made him waffles and had listened, delighted, as he re-enacted the break up that had occurred on the dance floor between the Prom Queen and the school's All-American quarterback. If Peter was as tortured as he later claimed to have been during those years, she had missed it, and knowing this now was just a further injury.

A friend of hers at church had a son who was a heroin addict, and Ruth thought of theirs as different paths in the same woods. Her friend had once confided that she hated to answer the phone late at night because she was certain it would bring word that her son had overdosed. Ruth could relate. There'd been years where she thought any day might deliver the news that Peter was dead from AIDS. She still didn't believe him entirely when he insisted that he was healthy. *Healthy and lucky*, was how he put it.

During her last chemo session, their pastor had sat with her for a few hours in the treatment room of Duke's Cancer Center, which seemed to her like Hell's version of a salon with its banks of salmon-colored recliners, its hovering, smocked volunteers offering reiki treatments and lemon water, and its bags of relentlessly bright drugs emptying drop by drop into her veins. "God's with you even when you're puking," he had told her. "Especially when you're puking," he'd corrected himself earnestly and she could tell he was pleased with himself for using such an earthy term as puking. Young, handsome and brimming with ambition to double the membership of North Baptist, he had a touch of the golden boy about him. But he wasn't quite prepared for the underbelly of the congregation's life. *Reverend Doctor Good Boy*, Ruth called him to herself, and she knew he was wrong about this one. She would allow that God was getting her through in a general sense, sure, but there was no way he had anything to do with the sour, fetid stench of chemo puke or the animal-like convulsions that could possess her body.

By the time Janet arrived that morning, Ruth had her wig and her fake boobs in place. Cheyenne they called the wig,

Pamela and Anderson, the boobs. The wig fell in a way her natural hair never had and the breasts were as perky as hers had been at twenty-five. She often kept her bra on during sex, for Ronny and for herself. It was just too much otherwise, the battered, stark flatland of her chest, the scars.

"You won't believe who I saw at the gym this morning," Janet began, pushing her sunglasses up into her newly-highlighted hair and reaching into the fridge for a can of Diet Coke. Through pilates and a raw foods diet, Janet had dropped four sizes and bought a new wardrobe in the past year. That her makeover coincided with Ruth's puffy-faced, bald-headed, flat-chested retreat from femininity was hard to miss. Maybe it was only fair, Ruth thought sometimes. She had always been the pretty one, the lucky one. She'd also been fertile and had chosen a faithful first husband. There had been reason for Janet to envy her. *You have no idea what it's like to know that you are completely alone. Even if something were to happen with you and Ronny, you'd still have Peter,* Janet had said years earlier, when they'd gotten drunk on gin and tonics the night her divorce went through.

"Ginny Murray." Janet answered her own question. "She got gastric bypass last year. Her belly flap is about down to her knees. I was next to her in the locker room and it took no less than five minutes to tuck that thing into her panties." Ginny had gone out with Ronny during the six months that he and Ruth had broken up during senior year of high school. Janet still delighted in any excuse to bring her up.

She and Ruth had been best friends since the age of seven. Janet had been there the day Ruth met Ronny, on their first day of junior high in 1966. Ruth had been maid-of-honor at both of Janet's weddings. Janet and Ronny alternated chemo shifts, so that Ruth never went alone. And the one time that Ronny had truly fallen apart, when Ruth was in the ICU with an infection almost too quick for Dr. Patel to contain, it had been Janet who pulled Ronny through. She'd found him about to peel out of the hospital parking garage, whiskey on his breath, fear in his eyes. She'd talked him into her car and back to her house, where her second husband had brewed a pot of coffee and made up the guest room.

"Pack a bag at least," Janet said when Ruth told her about Felix's call. "We'll go to brunch and see how you feel," she said, reaching to pull down Ruth's overnight bag from the top shelf in the hall closet.

When Janet had hit menopause, she had come to a tenuous peace with the fact that she would never have a child and something had changed, slowly but perceptibly. She remarried, choosing an unlikely man. Her new husband was an ex-hippie contractor who'd tripled his business during the building boom of the last decade. They bought a beach house and two Lab puppies who went to daycare when Janet had her weekly shift at a shelter for battered women. Her husband smoked pot and had coaxed Janet into joining him a few times. She had told Ruth it made their sex better, along with a dose of the big V. Ruth envied her sometimes.

"All I'm saying is keep your options open. I know he put you in a terrible position by not inviting Ronny. But you *can* go and that's the beauty of it." Janet adjusted her sunglasses in the rear view mirror and backed out of the gravel driveway. Ruth smiled as Buster charged the chain link fence and barked, slobber hanging from his gray jowls. An overnight bag, packed with her black cocktail dress, pj's and a change of clothes was in the backseat, along with Janet's gym bag and dry cleaning.

"What would I tell Ronny?" Ruth asked.

"He'll be so busy with his deer carcasses, he'll hardly know you're gone."

Ruth hadn't been on a plane in a decade. They preferred to travel by car. She'd seen and done what she wanted to in life. She could say that now. Fifth row seats to see Johnny and June Cash at the Grand Ol' Opry. Visiting the Vietnam Memorial with Ronny. Walking Foley Beach by moonlight on their 25th wedding anniversary. Staying at The Biltmore Estate, where they'd splurged on champagne and filet mignon from room service. It was a good life.

Janet ordered low-fat, low-carb everything at Atlanta Bread Company and Ruth sipped on a banana smoothie. They sat in matching faux leather armchairs. Sun streamed in through the large front windows, which allowed an unremarkable view of SouthPointe Mall's parking lot. SUV's and mini-vans circled the lot, screaming kids lagged behind their glaze-eyed parents, a skinny teenager in baggy jeans and a Carolina baseball cap stuck his hand in his girlfriend's back pocket and pulled her close. Something easy to listen to poured through the speakers.

Janet was eager to talk about her sister, Becky, who was staying with them and no longer speaking to her husband. "Becky said that *he* said that the trainer makes him feel alive. Well, sure you feel alive when you're having the sex of your life and you lose twenty pounds and a younger woman's throwing herself at you. This one, she used to be a cheerleader at State and apparently she's pretty acrobatic. I bet she's gotten him into some kinky stuff. That's one thing I'm trying to get through Becky's head. She's had a terrible time since Mom died. But you can't stop having sex with your husband for a year and then be totally shocked when this happens.

"A whole year?" Ruth asked.

Janet nodded. "She finally told me she's been suicidal from the depression. I had no idea. No one did, not even her doctor. Turns out she hasn't been sleeping for months either. I told her they can get through this, but she's not exactly in a conciliatory mood. Yesterday he showed up on the porch wanting to talk and she threw a shoe at him. It hit him in the forehead. I keep telling her, sweetie, it doesn't have to be so black and white."

"He took a vow," Ruth said. "They both did." She saw no need to dwell in the gray on this one. Even in her worst moments with Ronny this much was clear. *Don't cheat, don't split up.*

"Well, I'm taking her to the doctor tomorrow," Janet kept talking and Ruth's mind wandered, as it often did in conversations like this. She thought about how she and Janet used to walk from school to the Royal Ice Cream Parlor on Friday afternoons where they'd sip Cokes, smoke and wait for Ronny to finish his shift at his father's gas station. That was back when the downtown tobacco warehouses still churned out millions of Lucky Strikes each year and a few years after the sit-ins at Royal. She'd met one of the students who'd gotten arrested, a quiet girl with horn-rimmed glasses and braids who lived a few blocks from her. They'd once shared an umbrella as they both walked home in a May thunderstorm from their respective schools. The girl had grown up to be a law professor at Carolina and Ruth sometimes saw her being interviewed on the news.

Back then, she had thought she and Janet and Ronny would go on and on like that forever. Over forty years had passed. In some ways, so little had changed. They'd had one long run together. She wasn't going to get much more time. She knew that was true, although she didn't have the heart to tell Ronny or Janet or Dr. Patel. Before, she had been fighting. But now she was dying.

A man walked by holding a tray and a newspaper and when he turned to sit down, Ruth realized she knew him from church. He was the one who'd given that testimonial, though she could not place his name. He was sitting alone, sipping coffee and spreading cream cheese on his bagel. She watched him and she thought of Peter. Every few seconds, she gave Janet an "umhmm." Her friend was an endurance athlete when it came to talking. Listening to her often exhausted Ruth, but Janet's monologues never struck her as less than a feat.

The man glanced away from his newspaper, picked up his phone and then set it down again. There was that cocked quality to his wrist and his high cheekbones cast a slightly delicate quality to his face. But there was also the gold cross on a thin chain around his neck, visible in the v neck of his fitted t-shirt, and the matching gold band on his ring finger. Watching him, she looked for signs of happiness.

His phone rang and when he picked it up, he smiled, his shoulders relaxing, his eyes bright. He laughed into the phone and shook his head. Relief spread through her chest. She imagined his wife's bright voice on the other end of the phone, maybe telling him about her workout or calling from the grocery story to ask his opinion on wine. She watched as he finished the call, still laughing. He was finding a way through and this gave her hope. *This* was what she wanted for her son.

"Let's go to the airport," Ruth said, interrupting Janet.

Janet raised her eyebrows but Ruth was already up and clearing her tray. She knew now that she was meant to go to San Francisco. She wouldn't give up on Peter, but nor would she try to talk him out of the wedding. There was no need to. That was the great joke of it all, and she only wished she'd seen it earlier. The wedding wouldn't be legal or real and neither would the marriage. They were play-acting. *It's about performance.* Isn't that what Peter had said? Let them go through with it. Fine. It could be undone, like so much else. She would once again be by Peter's side, and from that position she could whisper to him that there was another way. It was all so clear. She felt a surge of energy and promise. As Janet rushed to catch up with her, Ruth laughed. The sun shone brightly and they had plenty of time to get to the airport. She was going to be with her son, like any mother would.

They pulled out of the parking lot and headed east on I-40. Ruth didn't tell Janet what had changed her mind. She didn't want anything to ruin this and knew the many ways that Janet could, with her bawdy humor or her occasional bursts of chilly, irrefutable logic.

They were two miles from the airport when they hit traffic. Above them, the silver bellies of planes angled towards the runway and the blue sky seemed endless. From behind, they heard an ambulance and fire trucks approaching. All the traffic inched left and Ruth watched as the emergency vehicles sped by. "Must be bad," Janet murmured, checking her watch. "But we've got lots of time."

The mid-day sun was blistering. It soaked Ruth through the windows of the SUV. The relief that she had felt was being replaced by a crawling anxiety. The seat belt was too tight against her chest, but she couldn't loosen it. Sweat gathered along her spine and her mouth dried out as suddenly as if it had been suctioned at the dentist's. She gripped the handle on the side door and tried to swallow the hot bile gathering in her throat.

"Pull over," she managed.

They'd been through this drill before. But this time they were in the center lane, boxed in by traffic on both sides with a mile to go until the next exit. Janet put on her blinker and cut toward the shoulder, but the driver of the semi on their right gave them the finger and inched up to block their path. Ruth tried to open the door, but couldn't manage the automatic lock button. She vomited, a burning liquid with clumps of undigested toast and streaks of bright red blood. The vomit splashed onto the dash and all over the front seat. She couldn't stop.

"Shit, shit, shit," Janet said, blasting on the horn and reaching into the backseat for her workout bag. She yanked out a towel and placed it on Ruth's lap, and then took hold of her friend's clammy hand. Ruth's face was the gray of wet concrete. Janet rolled down the windows. "We're going to the ER, asshole," she yelled. The semi's driver finally understood what was happening and cleared a path for them to the shoulder. Janet gunned the car. Ruth kept vomiting until only blood was coming up.

As soon as the triage nurse saw her, Ruth was rushed off for a CT scan and x-rays. Janet ran alongside her stretcher and when Ruth's wig slipped out of place, Janet gently took it off, stuffing it into her purse. They took her to an exam room next and a nurse, intern, resident, attending, and oncology fellow streamed in and out, conferring in loud voices outside the curtain.

It was almost noon when Dr. Patel arrived, wearing a pink golf shift and jeans and slightly out of breath. Ruth began to cry then. She was on an IV and had an oxygen canula in her nose. The soft whirr of the gas entering her body and the beeping of the monitors filled her ears. Dr. Patel took her hand. "It's scary, I know. But you're OK, Ruth. You're OK. All that Advil you were taking for the stress headaches got to your stomach, that's all." His lilting accent always distracted Ruth a little from the news he was delivering.

"Where's Ronny?" he asked.

Janet held up her cell phone. "Hunting," she said tensely.

Dr. Patel frowned slightly. "We need to admit you for observation tonight, Ruth. But this doesn't change anything. The chemo's working. We're going to beat this." Ruth nodded, too tired to ask any questions. Janet stared at her phone, as if sheer will might summon Ronny back to civilization.

Hours later, Ruth lay in a bed on the 8th floor of the hospital. The Durham sky was dark outside her window. The unit was chaotic with the sounds of the night shift. Nurses' voices drifted in from the hall. A patient called out that she had to pee. A local anchorman narrated the day's news on her sleeping roommate's TV. Janet was in a chair next to the bed, wearing scrubs that a nurse had loaned her to replace her bloody clothes.

Ronny was finally on his way, tearing down I-40 with a dead buck tied into the back of his truck, calling Janet every five minutes for updates. The plane she might have taken would have landed in San Francisco already. Three thousand miles away, Peter would be getting ready for the ceremony. Any last bit of hope he'd been holding onto would have been extinguished by now. She could see him blinking a few times and shaking his head, as if adjusting to the concept that he was now fully severed from his family. This was not true, but she knew he would see it that way.

She had been certain they would be a different kind of family. The kind that lives a few miles apart and celebrates every holiday, birthday and graduation together. But they weren't.

After almost forty years of marriage, even Ronny could still surprise her. There were places in him that she'd never find her way to. Peter had been born three months before Ronny got home from his final tour. Janet and her mother had coached her through labor and Janet had moved in with her for those first few months. They'd all driven down to Fort Bragg to meet Ronny's flight from Dover. He'd kissed her first, and had later told her that they'd reminded his platoon to greet their wives before their kids, not to screw up this one simple thing. They— Ruth, her parents, Janet, Ronny's father—had stood in a circle around him on the steamy black tarmac, forming a shield as he knelt down on his knees and cradled Peter to his chest for the first time. It was only when he'd taken Peter into his arms that he had started to cry.

Standing there that day, she'd seen their whole life together and she'd felt in command of their future. Ronny was finally home and they would raise their son together. Their world, fractured for this time, would be whole again. She'd glimpsed it all—Ronny's getting his college degree, Peter's first day of school, his basketball games, his high school and college graduations, his wedding, the children he and his wife would have, even the days he would bury Ronny, and then her. It was no more or less than any parent would imagine. Decades later, when she would scour her memory for evidence of some arrogance or recklessness on her part that could be to blame, this moment on the tarmac would still strike her as innocent, unimpeachable.

But the years had proven that they were meant for other things. Sometimes during treatment, she still allowed herself to imagine Peter by her side, talking about nothing more than the weather or a movie they'd both seen. She could see him next to her, down to the dark hair on his hands, the stubble on his cheeks. It bought her a few minutes of cheap, sentimental relief. It was a compromise position.

Cancer had been trying to kill her for eight years and yet she was still alive. She knew almost nothing of the man her son had become, and he even less about her. That's what was real. Lying there with the oxygen canula positioned awkwardly on her upper lip, forcing a cold gaseous stream up each nostril. Her husband on his way, her best friend at her side, her pastor on call if things got worse, her doctor a good man who would fight to save her once again. They weren't ready to lose her, not even close. But she could feel death in the room. She closed her eyes.

She needed her strength. Peter wasn't the only one capable of performing. To smile gamely in the face of grim odds, to be the canary racing through the mine's dark shafts while others stood at the entrance and cautiously peered in: these gifts, he had gotten from her.

CUSTODY BUS

When Carlos and I get together—which is sometimes every few weeks and sometimes every few months—we do it here, at the W Hotel where I've been taking reservations for the last five years. It's easy for me to score a good room when there's a last minute cancellation. I book it with the employee discount and we hole up with a bag of weed and a few bottles of wine. Tonight, we're in a suite on the 18th floor.

When you work in hotels, they lose their glamour real fast. You hear stories in the break room and you swear you'll spray everything down with Lysol before touching it. Carlos and I joke about everyone who's been in a room before us. It's like when we used to rent pornos and feel this weird mix of disgust and camaraderie towards all the people who'd already watched them.

After I clocked out tonight, I walked across the hotel lobby, which was crowded with guests at a wedding reception. The newlyweds were two guys this time, both beaming, one giddy and one freaking out about the flowers and wine selection. The lesbian best friend was arranging people for group photos and checking her watch like they were timing a NASA shuttle launch. I weaved past her to make the closing elevator doors. Carlos had called when he'd gotten to the room a few hours earlier and I knew that when I pushed open the door, he'd be stretched out on the bed, channel surfing and sipping a beer from the minibar. Just like I knew that when he saw me, he would look, but not leap, up. This is how it is with us.

It's only one now but Carlos has already been asleep for an hour, his legs sprawled like open scissors across the bed, the snake tattooed on his shoulder rising with each breath. I can't sleep. Every time I shut my eyes, it feels like an obese child is sitting on my chest. This happens sometimes. More lately.

We've been divorced for nine months now. "I'll always love you, Cassie," he said to me, "but I can't be married to you anymore." How's that for logic? When someone asks what happened, I say we spent the time we had together like a wad of cash. Some people get sixty, seventy years. Some people get one night. We got nine years.

"You know this isn't normal," Carlos will say once in a while, gesturing towards the hotel room and then the bed and then us. Early on, Carlos convinced himself that I never really learned the difference between what's normal and what's just getting by. He wanted to fix me, to undo the past like it was a matter of bending steel rods.

He grew up in the Central Valley with both parents and five sisters and his abuelita and about fifty cousins. They had family feasts every Sunday and took annual trips to Juarez to visit his dad's family. Now he's a sous chef at a restaurant in SOMA and takes karate. But his first love will always be sci-fi. If he'd had his way, we would have slept on Star Trek sheets. He's also very big into spiritual growth these days and has read just enough self-help books to conclude that I have abandonment issues and therefore act self-destructively to repel the people who love me.

Fair enough. But even he couldn't resist the stories that came of my childhood. The Custody Bus was his favorite. At parties, he'd feed me opening lines, play my straight man, laugh in all the right places. I'd be lying if I said I didn't miss that.

For two weeks in the spring of 1980, my father was a hero in Danville, Virginia. He got a citation from the Mayor, ended up on the front page of the local paper, and, after staying over for three consecutive nights, got back together with my mother for a trial reconciliation. A Virginia boy with a reed thin ponytail and a joint hanging off his chapped bottom lip, he was always squinting at the world from behind the wheel of his Chevy Nova. He wore faded Levis with a twenty-eight inch waist and carried a maroon Velcro wallet, thin enough to be empty, in his front pocket. In addition to me and the Nova, he had two friends, a rusted out motorbike, and a power saw.

There was an epidemic of divorces in Danville that year and most of them were nasty. In my fourth grade class, half of the kids' parents had split up and the other half was convinced their parents were about to. We regularly missed school to testify in court. The guidance counselor visited our classroom once a week to lead a divorce support group. She walked around the room tapping kids on the head and asking, *What animal do you feel like at your mother's house? What about when you go to Daddy's?* I sat at my desk, praying she wouldn't stop at me and chewing on erasers until they turned to powder in my mouth. Next to me, my best friend Wolfy picked at a wart on his knee until it bled.

My parents were pretty functional divorcees. If they crossed paths in town, they'd peck each other on the check and say hey. But I still ended up on the Custody Bus. It was the brainchild of Judge Argus, who was presiding over all the divorce and custody cases in the county. Just looking at him, you could tell how much he hated his job, the snarl of love undone; sob stories about working overtime, bounced checks, no-show babysitters, seduction, betrayal; the snotty kids sitting in his courtroom, choking on their Sears-bought dresses and clip-on-ties, watching wide-eyed as Mommy and Daddy flayed each other on the stand.

The idea behind the bus was simple enough. The court would enforce visitation agreements by providing transportation. It wasn't hard for him to get it off the ground. An out-of-commission transport bus was salvaged from the State Prison in Richmond. It was driven by an ex-warden who was retired on disability and owed Argus money on college football bets. The Judge recruited a cadet from the Police Academy to be the Bus Monitor and put him on the county payroll. Every Friday afternoon, the bus would pick us up from school and deliver us to our non-custodial parent's home or workplace. Sunday evenings, the bus would come back around and reverse the route. Any given week, there were about forty kids on the bus. I sat next to my best friend Wolfy in the third row from the back. The seats were hard and patched with duct tape and everything smelled like old metal and sweat.

The first time I told Carlos about the bus, we'd only been dating for a few weeks and we were drinking margaritas and eating shrimp burritos. I thought he'd laugh, the way other guys had. But instead, his eyes got sad and he leaned in to kiss me.

Now, we can't stay apart but when we're together, he circles me like I'm a wild animal, ready to tear his heart out. We end up like this, holed up in a hotel room because we both happened to be free this weekend, Carlos dead asleep, me wide-awake in the tub, adding butts to the coffee cup balanced on the soap dish. The water's scalding and I'm as pink and desperate as a boiling shrimp.

I left Danville four months after graduating, one of a handful of kids in my class who got out. With the money I'd saved from working at Shoney's, I took a Greyhound to San Francisco because it was as far away as I could get and plus I'd just read Kerouac. I rented a cheap room in a share on Alabama that should have been condemned. There were rats in the basement and squirrels in the walls and the paint was flaking so bad it looked like the place had a skin disease. Inside, everything had been installed backwards or upside-down by our stoner landlord. The faucet handles, door knobs, the rusty chain link fence out front. This was back before the dot.com boom, when you could still rent a room for $300 a month. It was a shitty arrangement, but it was mine, and when I had extra cash, I bought scented candles and throw pillows and ear plugs to block out the unbelievably loud sex one of my housemates liked to have. When I was broke, I stole industrial-size rolls of toilet paper from work and toothpaste and tampons from friends' bathrooms.

My first job was at a coffee shop on Valencia. From there I moved up to waitressing and that's how Carlos and I met, at a restaurant on Church that charged $20 for a plate of meatloaf. He was a prep chef who skateboarded to work and was obsessed with the knife set he'd saved up for. Mostly he was quiet, but ask him about those knives and he'd turn into an infomercial. After we clocked out, we'd sit at the bar, smoking and drinking whiskey sours. One night I told him he should shave his head; he was still parting it to the side, like his mother had combed it for him for a school picture. *Will you do it?* he asked shyly, and we went to a 24-hour drug store and bought some clippers and then headed back to the house he shared with some guys from the restaurant.

His bed was made with a plaid spread. His Adidas were lined up on a rack along with a pair of polished black dress shoes. A framed picture of his family sat on his dresser. The room smelled —no shit—like Lemon Pledge. Four years later, we got engaged. He worked extra shifts to save money for my ring and then he proposed at the restaurant where he was working at the time. He paid a buddy to serve us a four-course meal after the place closed and to cue "Born to Run" when Carlos got down on one knee.

Carlos was the one who urged me to track Wolfy down a few years ago. He couldn't understand why I didn't keep in touch with anyone from Danville. This from the man who still plays soccer once a week with some guys from his high school team and who just threw a bachelor party for his best friend from sixth grade. When I finally got in touch with Wolfy, he was living in Chicago with his girlfriend. They had a six-year-old son and were pregnant again. We talked for about an hour and he told me his dad was living a few blocks from them. "He's pretty much our nanny. He can't wait for the next one," Wolfy told me, laughing. When I asked about his mom, he paused.

"She died three years ago."

"I'm sorry."

"She had breast cancer. The crazy thing is, we were finally getting along again."

"Yeah," I said and he was quiet for a second and I felt a small crack spread through my heart. Later he emailed me some pictures of his son playing basketball. It was like staring at a photo of Wolfy from the year we met and pledged to be best friends forever.

Wolfy's parents had hooked up on the Dead circuit. He spent the first three years of his life at shows. They split up because his Mom had an affair with the guitarist in a local Stones cover band, the one who thought he was Keith Richards. Wolfy's dad, AJ, was my dad's best friend and, for awhile, he was known as the only black Deadhead in the South. But when Wolfy's mom left him, he denounced the whole scene as a cult and forbade Wolfy from saying Jerry Garcia's name. He stopped wearing patchouli, bought a leather jacket, and started listening to R&B.

After their respective divorces, my dad and AJ moved into a one-story cinderblock house behind the Piggly Wiggly. On weekends, my dad slept until noon and when he'd finally get up, he'd have sour breath and head right for the shower, where he'd belt out Dead songs to piss off AJ. He'd walk out of the bathroom with a faded beach towel wrapped around his waist, his skin pink from the heat, and he'd crack open a can of Mello Yello and eat a few dry handfuls of Captain Crunch. Then, the day could begin.

During the week, my mom dragged my ass out of bed every morning at 6:00 and deposited me at the kitchen table. I'd wake up to find myself nose to nose with a bowl of soggy cornflakes, hearing my mom quiz me on spelling words as she packed bologna sandwiches and a couple of cookies into wrinkled brown bags for our lunches. She called us "The Girls," saying it like we were a team of superheroes instead of a skinny nine-year-old with glasses and an overworked nursing assistant about to spend her day taking care of a woman with Alzheimer's who thought it was 1970 and mistook my mom for her husband.

As far as my mom is concerned, everything that happened during that time was further evidence of what was wrong with my father. But Carlos hears something else in this story, something that appeals to his vision of the world as a place in which it is still possible to protect those you love, a place closer to his outer space utopia, where love and righteousness conquer all.

"Which little pisser's running his mouth?" the driver on the Custody Bus used to shout, barely audible over the rumble of the diesel engine. He glared into his rear view mirror and scanned our faces, swerving dangerously close to an idling cement mixer. Wolfy looked at me and crossed his eyes. I giggled. The Bus Monitor glared at me and shifted his weight to emphasize his holstered gun.

The whole thing was a nightmare. But Wolfy was the only one who seemed to grasp this. Once, shortly after AJ had read us a story about Rosa Parks, Wolfy staged a sit in on the bus steps. He refused to move and started singing "We Shall Overcome" until the Monitor grabbed him by the collar and deposited him in a front row seat.

Wolfy deserved a better sidekick than me. While he was up front, I sat in the back and stared out the window, watching the houses we passed, imagining what it would be like to have my own bedroom. The forces at work in the world seemed vast and beyond comprehension.

Every Friday, Wolfy and I were dropped off together at the garage where our fathers worked. They talked constantly about opening up a specialty shop where they'd only work on Corvettes, Mustangs, and TransAms. Their dream was to break into NASCAR. My dad wanted to be a driver, AJ his pit crew chief. The local track, which we visited every Saturday of the racing season, was one of the few places where my Dad seemed fully alive, like the smoke had finally cleared from his brain and, in the wattage of all those lights, he liked the version of the world he was seeing. He'd hold my hand and tell me every goddamn thing there was to know about those cars. The busted exhaust system that made #6 drop out of the race. The new engine technology in #42. We'd time how long it took the pit crews to change tires on my digital watch and if I picked the winning car, we'd head to the snack bar. "That's my girl," he say, peeling a five out of his wallet and pointing toward the handwritten, chalkboard menu of cotton candy and corn dogs as if he was offering me the world.

After the races, they'd take us to Catahoulas, the bar of choice for anyone under forty in Danville. While our fathers played pool, Wolfy and I would sit at the bar. He could blow a long rope of snot in and out of his nose and I could wiggle all my loose teeth with my tongue so that they bled.

My parents met at Catahoulas when they were eighteen. Under different conditions, my mom wouldn't have looked twice at my father. But the bar was his habitat. He shone there, a wizard at the pool table, quick to lay down cash for a round of drinks and quarters for the jukebox. I can see her at the bar, sipping a piña colada, watching him from behind her feathered bangs, taking note as he tapped his pool stick on the cracked cement floor to the beat of yet another Zeppelin song.

When my mom got pregnant six months later, he wanted her to get an abortion. This was 1971, and he went so far as to find the name of a doctor in Richmond. They broke up for the second trimester. Then one night, he showed up at her parents' house with a ring. Two weeks later, they were married at the Baptist church my mom grew up in, their families and high school friends looking on with strained cheer.

It took eight years for things to fall apart. More and more often, my dad stayed home when my mom and I went bowling or grocery shopping. Then he stopped being home at dinner, and then he came by one night with AJ's truck and loaded up a few boxes of his clothes, tools and records. I watched him from under the kitchen table and even when he crawled under there with me, I wouldn't talk to him.

It must have been harder than that. But I don't remember any fights or screaming. It was as if, at roughly the same time, they both understood that their love had run its course. Words like *eternal* and *permanent* weren't part of their vocabulary.

It's not like I didn't think about all this as I walked into the courtroom nine months ago, done up in fake pearls and that ugly navy blue dress my lawyer made me buy. Something inside of me turned to ash when I saw Carlos sitting shoulder to shoulder with his lawyer, his mother and two of his sisters right behind him in the front row.

"You don't deserve him," his older sister said when she cornered me in the courthouse bathroom during a break later that morning. "We're family people," she said, staring at me in the mirror and scrubbing her hands like she was getting ready for heart surgery. "And you don't pull shit like this with family."

I stared back as I put on fresh lipstick. In my head, I was calling her a piggy-faced bitch and thinking what a goddamn relief it was that I'd never have to sit through another one of her kids' first communions or confirmations, or listen to Carlos' diplomatic end of the conversation the next time she called to whine about some family drama. But I didn't say a word and she finally left. By the time I walked back into the courtroom no one could tell I'd been crying.

I was wiggling my three loose teeth for Wolfy when his mother knocked on the door of the Custody Bus. We were stopped at a red light a few blocks from the garage. The bus was already half-empty. The driver recognized Wolfy's mom and pushed the door open with a whoosh. She climbed up the steps, making room for a woman I recognized as Wolfy's aunt.

"We've been chasin' y'all all over town. I forgot to pack Wolfy's inhaler. Lemme give it to him real quick," his mother called up to the driver.

Next to me, Wolfy turned the color of redwood. He didn't have asthma.

The driver hesitated. But the women were already in the bus, lugging brown shopping bags with them.

"I'll get it to him," the Bus Monitor said, extending his hand. He was standing in the middle of the aisle, blocking her view.

"Wolfy! Come here, honey." Her voice sounded strange, like she was high on something she wasn't used to taking.

Wolfy stepped into the aisle and inched forward like he was walking the plank. When he got to the front of the bus, his mother bent down and whispered something in his ear and then nudged him, more forcefully than she needed to, into a front row seat. Suddenly the Bus Monitor doubled over and grabbed his crotch and Wolfy's aunt unsheathed a ten-inch hunting knife, its blade flashing. His mom reached into her shopping bag and whipped out a cordless power drill. She turned it on and pointed it in the direction of the driver. The light turned green, but we didn't move. The power drill inched closer and closer to the driver's face and Wolfy's mother ordered him out of his seat. Her sister was waving the knife in a big circle, orbiting the monitor's head.

"You're shit outta luck, buddy," Wolfy's aunt said, flashing a weird grin. Watching her, you would've never guessed that she worked as a bank teller in Roanoke and lived alone with two cats. During the trial six months later, she sat next to her lawyer and wept.

The light turned red again and they used the time to handcuff the two men together and shove them into the front seat across from Wolfy. They didn't resist. They just sat there like the rest of us. Wolfy's mom got behind the wheel and floored it. His aunt stood guard over the driver and monitor. The bus was dead quiet.

AJ and my dad were in front of the garage, gliding chamois cloths over the hood of a red Camaro. They looked up as the bus approached and when we careened by, they must have caught a glimpse of AJ's ex behind the wheel. I can't imagine that it took them long to figure out what they needed to do. They were men who had spent countless long, hot afternoons dreaming about unlikely scenarios involving heroics and fast cars.

I can hear AJ urging my dad on, cranking up the radio, bouncing in his seat like a kid. And I can see my dad nodding confidently and leaning closer to the wheel, sweat beading on his forehead as he became the man he'd always seen himself as. They chased us for miles.

I waited for the sirens, but none came. Dust circled the bus like a protective shield, pine trees racing by in a dizzying blur.

The engine sounded like it was about to explode and Wolfy's mother was practically kissing the steering wheel as she took it up to ninety. She was making a buzzing noise, like a cicada had taken over her vocal cords. The bus jerked violently as we rounded a corner. A kid behind me screamed. I hit my mouth on the seat in front of me and three bloody teeth landed in my lap.

Later, we'd be told that this was when the bus skidded off the two lane road, snapped a rusty barbed wire fence, got its fuel tank punctured by a fence post, and crashed into an abandoned barn. We'd learn that Wolfy's mother lost consciousness before the impact and that, upon impact, his aunt stabbed herself in the thigh. But in those moments, it was just a slow, blind terror, bodies sliding around the bus, the crimson of fresh blood and the dazzling shower of shattering glass, the sounds of tearing metal, someone crying, someone else cursing.

A few hundred yards back, the Camaro skidded to a stop on the side of the road and our fathers sprinted towards us. I pocketed my teeth and turned towards the rear door. None of the kids had been badly hurt and we all began lining up single file, facing the back of the bus like we'd drilled for just this situation. My Dad caught each of us as we jumped off the ledge of the door, easing us onto the hard-packed red dirt and telling us to find a buddy and run to the Camaro. AJ was working the other end of the bus, wedging open the door and dragging Wolfy, his ex-wife and her sister away from the flames.

My dad and I were on the front page of the paper the next day. In the picture, his arm was around me and we were staring at the charred, smoky remains of the bus. He looked like the kind of man who would do anything to keep you safe.

The hijacking didn't make sense. After all, Wolfy's mom had primary custody and was going to get him back that Sunday. At her sentencing hearing, she stood up and said, "I'm sorry anyone got hurt, but sometimes you have to fight for the people you love." She was sentenced to five years but got out on good behavior after three.

My parents' trial reconciliation began the night of the high-jacking and lasted for two weeks, enough time for us to settle back into a routine and take a day trip to Virginia Beach. My mom and I spent most of the day sitting on the wet sand, letting the waves rush up over our legs. The surf was rough, and since my mom didn't know how to swim and I could only doggy paddle, we were scared to get in past our knees. My dad lay out on his Budweiser towel, his undershirt balled up over his eyes because he'd forgotten sunglasses, his pale legs sticking out of cut off jeans. Wisps of light blond hair ran down the center of his chest like a dividing line. He refused to put on anything but baby oil and over the course of the day we watched him turn brighter shades of pink.

Every hour or so, he'd prop up on his elbow and whistle at us. I'd turn around and wave. My mom would look at him, shake her head and smile like we had all the time in the world. We drove home late that night, stopping at Dairy Queen for dinner. I fell asleep to the sound of them laughing, the red glow of their cigarettes lighting the front of the car.

My dad took off again the next week. He called from the garage and told my mom he was moving back in with AJ. My mom didn't fight for him. She knew that the ride was over.

At parties, I leave most of this out. Then, it's just the stuff about Wolfy's sit in and the bus getting hijacked and all the press coverage. It's like the way, tomorrow morning, when we're sitting in bed eating room service waffles, I won't mention to Carlos that I spent half the night in the hotel tub like this, wanting to be alone and also wanting him to wake up and find me.

My dad left Danville when I was twelve and moved, in

quick succession, to Atlanta, Daytona Beach, and finally Charlotte, where he got his first job on a NASCAR pit crew. First he stopped visiting. A few years later, the calls and postcards stopped too. For a while, I used to fantasize about his kidnapping me. I wanted him to be an outlaw, to want me as badly as Wolfy's mom wanted him. That was before I knew that he had never asked for full custody.

My mom and I talk three or four times a week and I go home at least twice a year. Every morning, she gets up at 5:30 to fix breakfast for her husband and get ready for another day of caring for strangers. It's been almost twenty years since I've heard from my father. He missed my high school graduation, my wedding, my thirtieth birthday. If I ever have kids, he'll miss them too. It's almost like he's dead, except I have no idea where he is. I still think about him, though. That's how the ones that disappear get you. I imagine him spending every day at the track, hustling to change a tire and watching his driver circle the track, finally in love enough with something to stick around.

When Carlos left me, I cried so much that I got dehydrated. No shit. They had to give me an IV at the emergency room and even when I was sitting there watching the bag of saline slowly empty, I couldn't stop crying. They wanted to keep me overnight because they thought I was a suicide risk.

I cheated. With a guy named Luis. He's works here at the hotel. He wears a wedding ring, but he's not married. It belonged to his father, who died a few years ago. He's a good guy and he moonlights here to send money home to his mom in Argentina. I never loved him. It was Carlos I loved. I wanted Luis, though, and he wanted me back.

We'd sneak into empty rooms and the sex was better than it had any right to be. It lasted six months before Carlos found out. We made it through three appointments with a therapist and, at his mother's insistence, one session with a priest. Then he left.

Maybe it is just getting by, this arrangement we have. One night at a time, every few weeks, only at the hotel. We had room service tonight, though I had to make sure it wasn't Luis who delivered. Afterwards, we watched the sun set over the bay. I counted the white sailboats to distract myself from how high up we are. But the higher, the better for Carlos. He leaned against the window like he was ready to leap into the sky. I wanted to pull him away from it.

"I met someone," he said, staring at the water.

"Then why are you here?" We had agreed not to talk about stuff like this.

"Because she's not you, Cassie." He still wasn't looking at me.

I touched the snake tattooed on his back. "Hssssttt," I said.

He finally turned around.

"Come home," I said.

He looked me in the eye, but he didn't say anything, and then we went to bed. For a few months, Carlos wouldn't touch me, and then he would, but he'd keep his eyes closed, and then he'd open his eyes but still not talk.

But tonight, it was like it used to be. He likes me to straddle him and take his dick in my hand like it's a steering column. That's his term not mine, as in the manual steering column of the *Starship Enterprise*. "Call me Pavel," he said in a cheeky Russian accent. "Ensign Pavel Chekov," I cooed and he grinned and got harder as I steered him, and then he closed his eyes and arched his back. *You know this ain't normal, baby?* I whispered into his ear and, that quickly, he winced and went limp, staring at me like I was a stranger. I could see his brain working, choosing what to do next. My stomach dropped, but I didn't say anything and I didn't move. My thighs clenched his hips and I could feel the pulse in his groin beating against my skin. A second passed and then a few more and it felt like the whole tangled history of our nine years together was in bed with us. Finally, he put his hand on my stomach, the way I like. "No one's ever gonna love you like I do, Cassie," he said and then pushed me onto my back and rolled on top of me, his hands clenching my wrists, his eyes wide open.

AN EQUAL AND OPPOSITE FORCE

In early May, Doctors Reddi and Lombardo shocked each other by confessing that they had fallen in love with the same woman. That Reddi and Lombardo were best friends and that this woman, Erin Champion, had been married to another woman for six years meant that it would be a difficult season for all of them. They knew this, and yet they could not help themselves.

A year earlier, Raj Reddi and Miles Lombardo had co-chaired the search committee that lured Erin to Berkeley from her tenured post at MIT. She was a headliner at conferences and a go-to talking head for NPR and CNN when something notable happened in physics. For three years running, *The Advocate* had named her one of the nation's twenty sexiest gay scientists and doctors.

When he called to invite her for an interview, Lombardo knew all of this. He'd also heard that she was ambitious and prickly, and that she slept with students. Erin handled that first conversation diplomatically, though it couldn't have come at a better time for her. Yes, she would fly out for an interview. She was intrigued by the invitation, she said, and she'd been following their work—his particularly—for years.

When Lombardo met her at the airport a week later, he saw that she was more beautiful at close range than she was behind a podium or on television. Her hair was short, dark and stylishly cut; her eyes were green, her skin tan and her cheekbones high and defined. Introducing himself, he wished his palms didn't sweat, and he wondered if she'd ever been with a man. Her manner was crisp, just shy of unfriendly. As they walked through the dark corridors of the parking garage, he quickened his pace to match hers. Her body was like a distance runner's.

That night, Reddi and Lombardo took Erin to dinner at Chez Panisse and each man observed that when she laughed, she closed her eyes and her face softened. Into their third bottle of wine, she began calling Reddi and Lombardo "the boys" and, in response, they began blushing. It took another two weeks to finalize her contract.

When she arrived in August, Erin was assigned a corner office in LeConte Hall, a few doors down from Reddi's. On her first day, she beat him in. Walking down the second floor hall at 6:30, he was met by the sound of jazz and the faint smell of her dog, a shaggy, gaseous mutt that she seemed inordinately fond of. Unlocking his door, Raj grimaced. He had always been the first one into the department and he loved having those hours to himself. But he knew what was necessary. He knocked on her door and greeted her cheerfully; he made sure she knew where the copier and the faculty kitchen were. He told himself he would learn to share what he had always guarded closely.

By the start of the semester, Reddi looked forward to their morning routine. They'd begun having breakfast together in her office once or twice a week. The first few times, he'd eaten quickly, anxious to get started with his work. But when he started to excuse himself, she would insist that he relax and finish his breakfast. Sometimes, they traded food. Half of her blueberry muffin for a few bites of his egg sandwich, her banana for his lemon yogurt.

At first, she thought that he was gay and this had pleased her. She had never had an out colleague before. But after several weeks with no mention of a boyfriend, past or present, she decided he just didn't know yet that he was gay. Perhaps she could coach him along. But when he started mentioning the dates he went on most weekends, she realized that he was something of a catch among women on campus.

As the weeks slid into months, Raj began pushing himself on his morning runs, getting to work fifteen minutes earlier in order to arrive as Erin did and walk in with her. After awhile, it seemed to him that they had always eaten breakfast together and it became easy to imagine sharing dinner with her too. Her office was warm and bright with morning sunlight. Just a semester into being there and already it was better decorated than his. Two abstract paintings by her wife—slashes of red against a black background that struck him as unnecessarily severe—hung over her desk. Her bookshelves were filled and an orange and red Navajo rug covered much of the floor. They would eat at the coffee table near the door, Raj perched on the buxom love seat, Erin in a leather smoking chair, her legs crossed at her knees. Sometimes it was hard for him to reconcile this more intimate side of her with the aggressiveness on display in faculty meetings, but he didn't dwell on this.

"You have a bit of yogurt," Erin said one morning in January, gesturing towards Raj's moustache. He wore a beard that was always in need of a trim. He wiped his mouth with the back of his hand, embarrassed. "I've heard that men with beards are hiding something," she went on.

He laughed and shook his head. He'd never thought much about his beard; he had grown it because his father had one. But that night, as he stood in front of his bathroom mirror with scissors and a newly purchased electric razor, it was easy to imagine Erin's looking up from her desk and smiling at his naked face. It didn't occur to him that she'd hardly notice at all.

Raj had spent a good deal of his adult life recovering from being a prodigy. At two, he was doing subtraction and addition problems at a table of delighted, clapping aunties in Delhi. When his father got a job in the math department at Duke, his family moved to the States. At fifteen, he was admitted to Duke and lived at home during the three years it took him to complete a Physics degree. At twenty-three, he defended his dissertation on the deep inelastic scattering of electrons on protons.

He made it to thirty before he knew what failure felt like. That year, his third at Berkeley, his lab was the second one to produce experimental evidence of the quark. They published only two months after the team of physicists at Stanford that went on to receive the Noble Prize. Eight weeks. Not even sixty days. Nothing at all for a man used to contemplating the nature of time.

He punished himself for months afterwards, calculating all the ways he'd wasted precious hours that year. The desire for sleep he had indulged; that goddamn movie he'd gone to because it was a rainy, dark night and he'd allowed himself to feel lonely. It wasn't until his early thirties that he began to ponder his own happiness or that he asked a woman on a date.

**

Erin's world was different than Reddi and Lombardo's. She and Jane, who was still living in Cambridge, had an open marriage. Erin maintained, in both conviction and practice, that only the vestiges of Victorian ideals stood between most people and the great barrels of fun to be found in polyamory.

When she came out at seventeen, her parents kicked her out and she moved into her girlfriend's University of Georgia dorm room. Considering it a question of survival—or not—she had cut all ties with her family, Pentecostals who didn't tend to drive past the county line except to attend revivals. Erin didn't talk about her childhood, except to Jane. Those who paid close attention, usually the women who came and went from her life in a matter of months, glimpsed evidence of her wounds in the numbing third tumbler of whiskey she opted for on many nights. But this too, Erin explained merely as a matter of preference.

She was self made and she'd done what she set out to, getting tenure at thirty-five, her research progressing, a house in Cambridge that she and Jane restored, a month in Provincetown every summer. She'd endured the battles and slurs of the 90's, and countless run-ins with the old guard at MIT, fossilized men who'd worked under Einstein and lunched at the Faculty Club. But recent years had brought a different set of challenges.

The fall prior, Lucy had taken a front-row seat in one of her seminars at MIT. Every few weeks, Lucy would stop by during office hours, sitting close enough that their knees brushed when Erin leaned over to look at the younger woman's calculations. Erin had slept with students before, but not freshman, and not the daughter of a trustee. From the start, when they met for coffee in Central Square, Erin had made her terms clear. She was committed to Jane, she explained, and they were rock-solid. But she was available for sex and each moment that she spent with Lucy would be real and intimate. Polyamory was very Buddhist in this way, she liked to say, a corporeal primer in the abundant realities of the moment. To all of this, Lucy had nodded, as if she understood all there was to know about the human heart. She had reached for Erin's hand then and kissed the inside of her palm.

Erin booked a room for them at The Charles Hotel on Harvard Square, the first of many nights they would spend there. Jane knew exactly where they were and what they were doing. She knew Lucy's first name, but not her age. At the time, it had seemed to Erin a minor omission. Months later, when everything unraveled, it was those mornings in the hotel that she would think about. She would remember looking out at the early morning sun on the Charles, a rowing eight gliding over the water, the first time that Lucy said *I love you.*

I love you too, Erin had replied, because in that moment, she did. She loved Lucy's lean, tight body and the secrets that tumbled out in the dark. She loved how Lucy's long hair spread like a dark stain on the crisp, white pillow, how real heat passed between them.

But by March of that year, Lucy had become clingy and demanding, breaking down every time Erin wasn't available to see her, showing up at her office, her lab, and even one time her doorstep. *You've got to end it,* Jane said, and then added, *she's a grad student, right?*

Erin broke it off during Reading Week. Lucy failed an exam and ended up on suicide watch at health services, where everything came out. There was an internal investigation and then countless disciplinary meetings with her dean. Once the termination papers were drafted, the dean called Erin back in. "Her father has withdrawn his five-year pledge and threatened to resign from the Board of Trustees. He wants to pursue criminal charges, but the girl won't do it."

Erin had nodded, and she'd felt a stab of remorse that life had taken this turn.

But not even in the darkest lashings from Jane—*Almost forty and still, you're an infant. You can't stand that anything would be off-limits to you. She was raped by her high school Physics teacher and then she stumbles into your classroom a year later. And don't you dare start that bullshit about how sex with you somehow healed her. I knew you could be reckless, but this . . .*—had she felt genuine regret.

With her final day at MIT looming, Erin buried herself in her research, slept in the guest room at home and hacked away at the list of chores and repairs she otherwise rarely made time for. For those two weeks, she was an Eagle Scout. And then the call from Berkeley came. Between the package they offered and the 3,000 miles of distance from Cambridge, it presented an elegant escape route. MIT cooperated. Jane refused to even discuss moving with her, but they didn't go so far as calling it a trial separation.

That Jane still wasn't talking to her in any substantive way might have worried someone else, but Erin insisted that this was simply another phase of their life together. She was taken by the idea of the big, blank slate of the West. She rented a two-bedroom apartment a mile from campus and stayed late at her lab most nights. Every few weeks, she went into the city for a dinner party, having renewed a few friendships there. There'd been only one date though, with a recently single and sleep-deprived doctor whom she'd met at one of these parties. The woman had gotten drunk on two glasses of wine and insisted on telling a drawn out version of her break up story about an ex who was already pregnant with another woman. During dessert, Erin went to the bathroom and when she returned, the doctor was asleep, a strand of drool dribbling onto her crème brulee. It was one the worst dates Erin had ever been on. She hadn't even bothered to explain about Jane.

By February, Erin felt settled into the department. Her lab group was congealing, the dean was pleased with her work, and she was building alliances with Reddi and Lombardo. She and Miles were co-advising a student and co-chairing a committee. At his suggestion they met for lunch once a week, usually at a diner near campus.

Their student was struggling to meet deadlines. His wife was pregnant with their second child and on bed rest. As they discussed this one afternoon, Lombardo looked down at the remnants of his cheeseburger. "My wife died when she was four months pregnant. It was the first year of my post-doc," he told Erin. He had not meant to confess this, but he had found that it was disarmingly easy to talk to her.

"I didn't know," she murmured. "I'm so sorry." She reached across the table and lightly touched his hand. Miles jumped and then mumbled an apology. When he looked up, he saw real concern in her eyes.

Miles thought of himself as a romantic brooder, but he didn't look or dress the part. He was 6'2" and underweight by ten pounds. He wore his hair, still jet black, in a blunt, Roman cut. His cheeks were pocked from acne scars and he favored jeans and turtlenecks, an ensemble that had served him reliably for twenty years. He had grown up in Buffalo, the only child of a municipal worker and a secretary. His parents were as proud of him as they were baffled by him. He was driven and outspoken; there had been a few bar fights in high school and during his undergrad years at Syracuse, and then an arrest for drunken and disorderly conduct the month after the accident. Even now, he was unable to entirely control his temper.

He had arrived at Berkeley when he was thirty-two, his seventh year as a widower. At first, the Bay Area irked him. He missed the big, walloping storms that dumped a foot of snow on Buffalo and, months later, the blazing heat of July. He couldn't locate a single Bills fan on campus and he found that women and men alike maintained eye contact for too long. Not to mention how eager everyone seemed to talk about their chakras and how cavalier they were about the earthquakes that shook the city every few months.

For the first few years, every seismic event had rattled him. With each one, his stomach dropped and he was convinced that it was the Big One. At a dinner party once, the table started to shake and his wine glass tipped over. He leapt from his chair and huddled in a doorway, his hosts and date still seated and trying not to laugh at him. He felt justified, though. The data was unambiguous. It *would* happen; it was simply a question of when. In time, though, the element of surprise wore off and he understood that he couldn't maintain a state of constant vigilance. Besides, could whatever nature had in store for them really be more harrowing than the hell he'd already survived. He still flew out to Syracuse once a year to visit his parents and Lily's grave, but Berkeley became his home. He bought a sunny duplex a few blocks off Shattuck that he filled with plants, Scandinavian furniture and an encyclopedic collection of jazz cds.

**

Their meals with Erin rounded life out for both Raj and Miles, who otherwise relied mostly on each other for companionship. They'd been best friends for a decade and every Friday played squash on the RSF courts. After these games, they showered in a little-used faculty locker room and walked three blocks to Beckett's Pub on Shattuck where they sat at the bar, ordered stouts and talked about work, politics and women. It helped their friendship that they were different kinds of physicists. Lombardo was a theorist who had spent the past twenty years working on the theory of cosmic turbulence. Reddi was an experimentalist and his lab was racing five others around the world in the quest to either disprove or confirm the universality of gravity.

Three years earlier, when Raj's mother died, he'd broken down at the bar. Lombardo had offered him a pile of crumpled brown napkins and he had placed his hand on his friend's shoulder. For a moment, it felt as if his body was a shield between Raj and the rest of the world, and then the moment passed.

More and more, they talked about Erin as they sipped these Friday beers, but neither confessed his growing feelings for her. They compared notes on the rumors they'd heard about her marriage and they agreed that it sounded like the kind of adaptation a good scientist would come up with. Look at the data around infidelity and divorce. Clearly monogamy wasn't an elegant solution to human needs. Why not experiment? Watching his married friends, Raj saw parts of them diminished, parts of them enlarged, sometimes grotesquely.

"Why do it?" he asked Miles.

"Love, man," Miles had said, draining his Guinness and signaling for another.

Besides his mother and sisters, Raj had never said I love you to anyone. But Lombardo had no doubts about the name for his feelings towards Erin. He had fallen like this once before, when he met his wife, Lily, at twenty-one. Four years later, she was dead and Miles took a leave of absence from his program, retreating to his parents' house in Buffalo for a full semester. Three times, his mother dragged him to see the priest at Immaculate Conception, who urged Miles not to dwell on the fact that he had been driving, that he'd had three glasses of wine with dinner, that he'd gotten off with a broken collar bone and five stitches on his chin. But for Miles, forgiving himself was out of the question.

Erin wasn't oblivious to the effect she was having on her colleagues. As February and March rolled by, Raj began finding excuses to pop his head in her door and frequently forwarded her articles about subjects they'd discussed over breakfast. Then one evening, he stopped by her office to ask if she wanted to join him for a drink. She smiled and declined, telling him she was on deadline. But the next morning, when they would have normally had breakfast, she came in late. When she and Reddi passed in the hall that week, she was abrupt. When he worked up the nerve to ask if this change in her schedule was permanent, she merely shrugged, as if it couldn't have been less consequential; stung, he nodded and walked away.

A few days later, Erin got an email from Lucy, who had transferred to Stanford and wanted to see her. Also in her inbox was a message from Jane, filling her in on the details of a furnace repair. She minimized her inbox, worked on a paper for thirty minutes, and then responded to Lucy's email, offering to drive down to Palo Alto for dinner and booking a room for them at a hotel a few miles from campus.

They met at a sushi restaurant that night. Lucy had cut her hair, gained ten pounds, and gotten a tattoo on her shoulder, familiar signs to Erin that she was coming out. Erin wanted to reach across the table and touch her hand, but knew that she needed to wait. They drank sake and slowly, Lucy began to relax and to eat rather than pick at the sushi on the shared plate between them. *I've missed you*, Erin said finally. Lucy popped a slick piece of eel into her mouth. She stared at Erin as she slowly chewed and then swallowed.

**

Weeks passed. The temperature rose. Trilliums and plum blossoms bloomed. Erin flew to Boston for a long weekend, during which she finally persuaded Jane to come out for a visit. The night Erin returned to Berkeley, Lucy drove up from Palo Alto. They'd decided to spend a full week together.

On Thursday morning of that week, Erin slipped out of her apartment before Lucy woke up, leaving a pot of hot coffee brewing and a bowl of strawberries in the fridge for her. She got to the office thirty minutes before Raj. He arrived full of resolve not to miss her, not to get up from his desk every time he heard a sound from the hallway. But as he rounded the corner, Raj saw the warm glow of light from her office and he heard her dog's nails hobbling down the hall. His stomach jumped and his pulse raced. He steadied himself and then knocked lightly on her door. Erin looked up and her face opened into an easy smile. "Come in," she said, raising her coffee mug as if to toast him. Stepping into her office, Raj blushed and smiled back at her. They drank coffee and talked about rumored cuts in the departmental budget.

The next morning, Friday, they had breakfast again and she laughed so hard at his impression of their dean that she nearly choked on her muffin. She mentioned to Raj that she was heading to a bed and breakfast in Mendocino for the weekend, but not that Lucy would be with her.

In the early afternoon, she met Miles for lunch. When he proposed that they co-author a paper, Erin agreed immediately. Without thinking, she dipped a french fry from her plate into the pool of ketchup on his, and, when they finally left the diner, she insisted on paying the bill. Miles took note of these details. Twice that afternoon, he picked up the phone to invite her to dinner and then stopped short. Don't rush it, buddy, he coached himself.

By 5:00 on Friday evening, Miles and Raj were well into their first game of squash and Raj had surged to a 12-3 lead. At game point, he lunged for a shot, the muscles of his calves straining against his brown skin. Miles took a step back and for a moment watched Raj instead of the path of the ball. He paid with the point and the game. Miles scowled.

They went on like this, Raj building up a lead, Miles cursing and occasionally throwing his racket. Raj waited these tantrums out and his game improved. Halfway through the second game, Miles settled into a rhythm with his swings and, after an hour and a half of play, edged Raj out.

"That was quite a comeback," Raj said as they stepped off the court and into the narrow hallway.

"You blistered me in that first game," Miles said, wiping his dripping forehead with the bottom of his t-shirt. He was slightly distracted, imagining what it would be like to go home to Erin that evening. To share this minor, amateur victory with her, to feel her hands rubbing the tight muscles in his back. He had been certain she'd felt what he did over lunch, the growing intimacy, the rising tension.

Both men were still sweating heavily when they reached the old faculty locker room. They were, as usual, the only ones there. The lockers were spotted with rust and the wooden benches were smooth with age. Exposed pipes rain along the ceiling and pale green paint was chipping off the cinderblock walls. At their lockers, Raj took off his drenched shirt, exposing his flat stomach and smooth chest. Miles felt suddenly restless and agitated, as if there was somewhere he needed to be. But there wasn't. He had begged off dinner with his cousin in the city; there was a cocktail party he'd been invited to, but the host was a great bore and he'd be the only single person there.

Their backs to each other, each opened his locker. "What would you do if you fell in love with colleague?" Miles asked.

"I'm flattered," Raj said.

"I'm serious. I need some advice." Miles combed through his gym bag for his shower supplies.

"Is it Erin?" Raj asked as he unbuttoned his tennis shorts.

Miles hesitated. "You talk with her a lot, don't you?" he askd.

"Not so much recently," Raj replied. His felt the cold weight of dread as he realized what had happened and exactly what it would mean to Miles. He wrapped his towel around his waist and walked towards the showers.

"Does she ever mention me?" Miles asked.

Raj said nothing as he turned on the water and waited for it to heat up. A current rushed along his spine and spread to his crotch. He knew this sensation. It felt as if Miles had beaten him to a discovery.

"She's a force, isn't she?" Raj said, stepping under the shower head.

Miles' flip flops slapped against the tile floor. He wore his towel around his neck and carried a soap container and a bottle of Head and Shoulders. "I couldn't hear you. I asked if she ever talks about me."

"Sure," Raj said, lathering his face.

"And?" Next to him, Miles fiddled with the handles. He liked to start his showers cold and work into the heat.

"And I guess the joke's on us," Raj said lightly, raising his arms and soaping his armpits and his chest. Wet and covered in green soap lather, he looked almost elfin.

"What are you talking about?" Miles said, staring at his friend. The cold water hit his skin like sleet.

"Well, for one thing she's married. To a woman. And for another, if she had to pick between us, she'd choose me."

Miles stepped towards Raj. "I just told you I love her," he said sharply.

"I know, Miles," Raj replied softly as he stepped out of the shower stream, his back pressed against the cool tile wall now.

But it was already too late. Rage was filling Miles and there was nothing he could do to stop it. He swung for Raj's face. It had been years since he'd thrown a punch and he slipped on the wet floor. His fist crunched into Raj's windpipe and then Miles' body crashed against him, slamming them both against the wall.

Raj covered his face and gulped for air. Soap dripped into his eyes and the sting was unbearable. He tried to push Miles off of him. But his hands were slick and Miles' long limbs were suddenly everywhere. For a moment, their bodies were pressed together. Raj felt something hard bounce against his stomach. It took a shocked second for him to realize what it was.

"Jesus, Miles," he said. He managed to push his friend away and then frantically splashed water into his burning eyes. He lifted his face to the shower head opening his eyes until the water worked the soap out. He turned, expecting to see his friend next to him.

When a minute passed and then another, Raj understood that Miles had left. He closed his eyes as the water pelted his body and the tile floor. He imagined Miles rushing onto the street and racing home, his body still wet under his clothes, soap in his ears and hair. He imagined Erin driving north along Highway One and because he could not help it, he saw himself in the passenger seat, his hand on her thigh.

He finished his shower, dressed quickly and walked towards his lab. Campus was quiet in that lull between dinner and the parties that would start in a few hours. A knot of students emerged from Bancroft, Ipod buds in, cell phones out. A jogger huffed past him; an aging Socialist extended a clipboard towards him, prattling on about another petition; an unleashed black lab loped across the green. Raj entered LeConte through a rear entrance and took the stairs up four flights. The wide halls were dark and empty. In his lab, he flicked on the lights and felt that same swell of anticipation that had been his companion since childhood. In this room—crowded but neat, equipment humming, a new report from the Lab Manager in his inbox— he could, quite literally, solve the mysteries of the universe. He would work through the night. He would be relentless. This time, he would get there first.

He sat down at his desk and fingered his neck and Adam's apple, tender and already starting to darken from Miles' punch.

He thought about calling his friend, but then didn't. Raj knew that Miles would be drinking wine, jazz blasting through his apartment, as glad as he was to be alone.

Just as he knew that eventually, they would act as if tonight had never happened, that privately each would find a way to account for this one outlying piece of data. They would lick their wounds and, in time, they would see how foolish they'd been to imagine futures with Erin, lives other than the ones they were clearly meant for.

He turned on his computer and clicked through to the newest data set. He stared at the numbers. Somewhere in them, an answer waited for him, coyly, impatiently, loyally. He thought again of Erin and Miles. No doubt, she would move on, and years from now, when her name happened to come up over Friday night beers, he and Miles would shake their graying heads and briefly consider all that might have been. He knew that, despite everything, they would never entirely regret the season that had just passed. Perhaps, he thought, they would even laugh about it one day, overcome by the absurdity, their faces red and contorted, their eyes filled with sudden tears.

MONKEY

Monkey craved privacy, fine bourbon, the first blast of steam at the gym, and the bodies of younger men. Each was available within a four-block radius of his place on Buena Vista Terrace, which he was finally getting retrofitted. Two weeks tops, he'd been promised when the engineer had unfurled the blueprint of his house on the coffee table and ticked off the structural adjustments they'd be making to the foundation and the cripple wall. Monkey had packed his laptop and suitcase and checked into the penthouse—the *Extreme Wow Suite!* the concierge insisted on calling it—at the W Hotel. But two weeks had dragged to three and then four, long enough that the doormen and room service staff at the hotel had learned his name.

Six months ago, he'd retired from the law firm he'd co-founded, getting out before the recession. Back in 2007, he'd warned the board that their projections for mergers and acquisitions were too aggressive, and they'd ignored him. But that was all in the past. Now he finally had time for long-neglected improvement projects—the retrofit, workouts with a trainer five days a week, Mandarin lessons in anticipation of a trip to China next summer.

He left the hotel at eight and took a cab to Gold's Gym in the Castro. Ryan greeted him outside the locker room and they started with twenty minutes of yoga and pilates. Ryan called this a spiritual tune-up; the flyers he posted at neighborhood coffee shops advertised his style as transformational. But most clients signed up because of his head shot on the flyer, which bore a passing resemblance to Brad Pitt, circa Fight Club. He knew his stuff though and in the six months they'd been working together Monkey had lost the extra fifteen pounds he'd been carrying since Dwayne got sick. He was down to an 8:30 mile and was training for a 10K at the end of March. His times were a far cry from the five-minute miles he'd logged when he ran for Harvard, but over four decades had passed since then.

After a set of intervals on the treadmill, Monkey's quads and hamstrings were burning. Ryan directed him back to the yoga studio, a room that lacked ventilation. One wall was covered by a mirror, the other was made of glass and faced the cardio room. Monkey felt like a hamster in a cage as he lay down on his back and caught his breath. Ryan tossed a medicine ball squarely at his chest. He raised himself to a sit-up position to catch it. Sweat poured down his face.

"One," Ryan barked. He checked his phone, smiled, and then pocketed it.

Monkey grunted, thrust the ball back at him and tried not to fart. "I worked Jack out this morning," Ryan said idly after a few more tosses, referring to the stylist that they both saw. He checked himself out in the mirror, adjusted his shorts and then chucked the ball back at Monkey. "And six," he counted. "Apparently he's single again."

"Umhmm," Monkey managed as the medicine ball landed with a thud against his chest. This time when he heaved it back at Ryan, he did fart, a quick, rank blast. Ryan caught the ball and raised his eyebrows. Monkey stared grimly at the leather ball hurling back towards his head.

Twenty minutes later, the workout was finally over and Ryan gave Monkey a friendly pat on the ass before heading off to his next client. Monkey downed a protein shake at the gym bar. In the shower, he shaved his chest and face and felt the welcome surge of endorphins kicking in. His mood was light as he dressed in the outfit he'd chosen for his noon haircut with Jack. Low slung jeans, a black button down and black loafers.

The cruelest part of aging was how easy it became to stumble unwittingly into humiliation. At sixty-six, he had made certain adjustments. He now favored suits with slim lines. So many of his cohort got it wrong, wearing jeans meant for twenty-five-year olds that simply drew more attention to their flat asses or holding onto pairs from the 90's because, by god, they still fit and that was something. It was the same with his hair. Although he was still in his late thirties, Jack understood all of this intuitively.

Monkey had been among Jack's first customers when he'd started cutting hair in the city fifteen years earlier. He'd been glad to circulate Jack's card among his friends and, more recently, glad again to be a silent partner backing Jack's salon. All of the details were handled through Monkey's financial advisor, but Jack found ways to thank him periodically. That winter he'd done hair at Fashion Week in New York and had brought back a tie from the new Armani collection for Monkey. For his birthday, Jack had given him a Kenyan wood carving of a monkey that he'd picked up at a small Parisian shop. It was no bigger than his palm and was one of the few pieces of décor Monkey had taken with him to the hotel. There, it sat on the living room mantle, its dark, curious eyes following him each morning and night. The gift had surprised him and moved him. No one had called him Monkey since Dwayne died. Somewhere along the way he must have told Jack about his nickname.

Since retiring, these appointments with Jack had become more of a bright spot in his calendar. He was still of counsel with the firm, but he rarely went into the office and he only stayed in touch with his former paralegal and the two managing partners he'd been closest to. It had been time to move on. Each new class of associates bored him more than the last; this latest wave had been a joyless Red Bull, vodka and Adderol crowd. They produced competent but uninspired legal work, clocking billable hours like they were advancing to the next level of a video game. Last year, not a single first-year associate had taken advantage of the free opera tickets that were available each month and he'd often sat next to an empty seat. Even the gay ones tired him, logging all of their pro bono hours chasing the right to marry. This hadn't kept him from inviting a few home in recent years, but it had lessened the thrill.

Other people, he liked very much and in a few cases, loved dearly. But since Dwayne's death four years earlier he had stopped socializing with those whose company he didn't enjoy. What a relief it had been, really, and his world had been both narrowed and improved. He was a good citizen: he dined with friends regularly and remembered their birthdays; he wore condoms; he made sizeable donations to a handful of organizations, although the checks now went to groups working in Tanzania and South Africa rather than the Castro and Chelsea. In this age, nothing stayed still, least of all a pandemic.

When he arrived at noon, Jack's salon was full, with three stylists and two colorists in rotation. The counters were burnished steel, the wood floors buffed to a high gleam. Monkey had helped pick out the Richard Prince cowboy print that hung in the waiting area. Jack was working on a woman's color in the back, but he looked up and smiled at Monkey, gesturing with his head towards an open shampoo chair. The receptionist, a whippet of a boy dressed entirely in white, brought him a glass of sparkling water with lime.

Sitting down, Monkey faced his own image in the mirror. Clean-shaven, his jaw line relatively firm, his eyes an unremarkable brown, his hair gray, but not white like Clinton's. How odd, Monkey thought, that Clinton was aging so well. Still a bit helpless with the big puff of bangs and the ill-fitting leisure wear, but the pink ties were cute and he was doing well for himself on the global stage. They hadn't seen each other in years, but it still pleased Monkey to see him redeemed.

"How are you?" Jack said warmly. His caramel-colored skin was darker from a recent vacation. He was wearing his hair tight these days. Monkey took in his narrow hips, the swell of his thighs against his jeans.

"Ryan had me doing intervals this morning," Monkey said "My hamstrings are a mess." He laughed and they chatted about their workouts as if they were members of a high school track team.

"You look terrific," Jack said. He billowed out the apron over Monkey's torso and clasped it tightly around his neck. A loose roll of Monkey's skin hung over the collar. Jack pushed his head under the warm water. The shampoo was cold and slick as Jack worked it into Monkey's scalp, his fingers efficient but not brusque. The cut itself took only fifteen minutes and left a spray of gray confetti on the floor. Jack held a mirror behind Monkey's head. This was all perfunctory, of course. Jack was very good and Monkey's hair had barely needed a trim.

Monkey stood up and smoothed the front of his jeans. "I'm still over at the hotel," he said. "Did I tell you they call the penthouse the *Extreme Wow!* suite?"

"Your place isn't done yet?" Jack frowned, impatient whenever he sensed incompetence.

"It's a nightmare. They call every day to say they've found something new to fix. The only thing that makes it bearable is the view from my hotel room. I look out at the Golden Gate Bridge."

Jack's eyes met his. A pulse of recognition passed between them.

"Come up tonight," Monkey kept his tone light. Usually in these moments what he had to offer was clear. He was the more powerful one, the better-looking one. But with Jack, none of this was true.

"*Tonight at the Extreme Wow Suite!*" Jack said. "It sounds like a Vegas show."

Monkey smiled. "I'll be back there by nine," he said, although he had nowhere else to be all day. "I'll tell the front desk you might be by."

Jack nodded but said nothing. The salon's phone was ringing. The whippet was watching them and then turned away, laughing too loudly at something. Jack glanced again at the woman whose hair was wrapped in foil. "Duty calls." He smiled.

"Of course," Monkey said, heading towards the door.

He had been rejected before, but he'd never felt a stabbing humiliation like this. He walked and walked, through the Castro, Dolores Park, into the Mission, up Bernal Hill, until he was out of breath and sweat spread across his back. Dwayne would have laughed with him and then comforted him. Dwayne who, at sixty, had become a child again. He kept a stuffed penguin nestled against his chest, giggled at cartoons, and tried to kiss all the male nurses and CNA's at the hospice. How odd that dying could allow you a glimpse of the child your lover had been, Monkey had thought as he'd smoothed the hair away from Dwayne's pale forehead.

They had met in their junior years at Harvard. At twenty, Monkey, still known as Douglas, was a classics major and escorted Jacqueline DeBussey to most formal functions. He was the treasurer of his fraternity and ran the 800 and mile for the track team, his body efficient, lungs burning, spikes chewing up the cinder. The first time he went to the park he was drunk. It was less than a mile from campus and, in those days, one of the better-known cruising spots in Boston. He circled its periphery, keeping his head down, his collar up against the October wind. That night, he didn't go in, instead returning to the warmth of his third-floor dorm room on the Yard. There had been a few trysts at Andover, the feverish pitch of his first time in a darkened science classroom with a young Latin teacher who'd served in Korea. But on that Cambridge night in 1963, he was still weighing his options. He played life with a strong hand, largely, he knew, because of his family's money. *America will fall before we do*, his father was fond of saying.

When he went back to the park a week later, Monkey understood that he was choosing the more arduous path; as he walked there, he had imagined with some prescience the nights he would later spend in Boston and Manhattan jail cells, the quiet payments that would be necessary, the growing weight of secrets in his life.

Beginning at nine o'clock, the police would patrol the park hourly, their boots slapping the sidewalk. At five-to, someone would whistle and the men would move to the trees. Up in the branches, Monkey would brace himself, his back against the trunk, its coarse texture cutting into his skin as his fingers dug into the hard thighs of his partner. The police kept their flashlights trained at knee-level and the bobbing circles of light would skim the park, illuminating piles of dead leaves, the pages of a newspaper, an empty pack of cigarettes. But the cops never looked up to see the ring of eyes staring down at them.

That he could travel among the trees earned him a reputation. Finishing with one man, he would creep to the end of the branch and swing easily to the neighboring tree. His record, in the time it took the cops to circle the park, was three trees, four men. It was Dwayne who first called him Monkey, tousling his hair with one hand.

A decade passed before they fell in love, though. After graduation, Monkey moved to New York for law school and Dwayne went to San Francisco to write. Over the years, there were a few letters between them, an unexpected run-in at a bar in the International Terminal at O'Hare. In 1972, Monkey gladly took an offer to transfer to his firm's new San Francisco office. The move released him from the endless social engagements of his clan - the foundation and charity events, the political fundraisers. He lacked his brother's avidity for these events as yet another occasion to show up in the Times or to corner a Senator and ask for a favor. Invariably Monkey would be out back smoking with the caterers, maneuvering for a quick fuck with the best-looking young man, just ten minutes in an empty study or bathroom, the boy's rented tux pants at his ankles.

He found that San Francisco was its own kingdom of meaning, a place that catered to the self-righteous and self-indulgent, he liked to say. But he loved it there and within a few years, he and two other lawyers had peeled off to start their own firm, taking a handful of major clients with them. It was in 1974 that he and Dwayne met again, at a New Year's party hosted by a mutual friend at his Marina condo. All night, Monkey had been restless. At quarter past twelve, he retreated to the foyer and located his overcoat in the front closet. Slipping into it, he paused briefly. Someone had said his name. But he ignored it and pulled his gloves on. "Don't go," Dwayne had called loudly, leaning over a steel banister, drunk and charming.

He stayed at the party. Dwayne went home with him that night and two years later, moved in. They were happy and it was simple. Not once did they discuss marriage. Dwayne would have scoffed at the idea.

They made it through the eighties. A goddamn harrowing time, when hospices were opening every few months and still turning people away. Several of his acquaintances and one dear friend had killed themselves in the seventies and it had been brutal. But this was on another scale entirely. He and Dwayne lost count at seventy-five funerals. It felt like everyone they knew was dying, and thus like the world itself was ending. But it wasn't. Go a few blocks in any direction and everything proceeded as normal. Monkey had become aware of how small their life actually was. Tiny, really. And yet, almost thirty years later, the virus had spread everywhere, and it felt like a cruelly powerful bond between his life and those of millions of strangers. *What kind of world is this,* Dwayne had asked once as they lay in bed.

In '93, Dwayne tested positive. It didn't matter how he got it; they agreed on that immediately. They had ten good years, time which they consumed like breathless, hungry kids, with trips to Tuscany, Paris, South Africa, Brazil. *The cocktails work until they don't,* Dwayne's doctor had said sadly as she wrote him a referral to the in-patient hospice on Church Street, unique because it doubled as a residential facility, a place where people might live for a few years before dying there. She was a young resident and Monkey had grown very fond of her. He had little interest in most of the lesbians he met; they were too serious, and either too easily injured or too intent on taking charge of a situation. But every so often one would charm him, and Dwayne's doctor had. She was campy, driven, bitchy, and looked like a teenaged boy; when her schedule allowed, she would visit Dwayne at the hospice, bringing him jelly beans and chocolate bars, watching cartoons with him. She and Monkey still stayed in touch.

For the two years that Dwayne lived at the hospice, Monkey had felt almost like a resident himself, experiencing that trill of anticipation when someone new moved in and the heavy weight of grief when someone died, taking sides, if silently, in the petty sibling bickering about who controlled the remote in the living room, who got an extra slice of chocolate cake at dinner.

We almost made it, Dwayne said in one of his last lucid moments. The night he died, Monkey held his hand and stroked his forehead and their friends came in one at a time to say goodbye. His nurse was there the whole time, monitoring the morphine drip and telling Monkey what each new symptom— the slowing pulse, the rales, the moment at which Dwayne sat upright and opened his eyes wide—meant.

Dear god. He could hardly stand to think of it, even four years later. After the funeral, he had thought seriously about moving back east. But he didn't want to leave the city Dwayne had loved so much. He still ate at their restaurants and had cocktails at the bars where they'd spent countless nights sipping martinis and commenting on every queen who passed by.

That afternoon he walked and walked, back through the Mission, past the Castro Theater and the bright boys in sleeve-less t's, distressed jeans and aviator glasses. He tried not to think of Jack, but it was hard to avoid. Monkey had known him since he was twenty-three, a young god who could get anyone he wanted. Somewhere along the way, he'd had his heart broken by a lawyer who'd gone back into the closet when he decided to run for office. Since then, there'd been a few other serious affairs and he'd had to bury several friends, losing them to overdoses and AIDS. By his early thirties—and right on schedule—Jack had found his footing. For all these years, Monkey had been a quiet but ardent observer, and when the time was right, he had let Jack know he would back him. But for all the obvious reasons he'd never made a move.

Now that he had, he felt like a fool. He replayed the con-versation again and again in his mind. That moment of eye contact. Jack's tone. That smile, as light as a lemon rind. He had not said yes or no. Monkey knew that Jack had been with older men, guys ten or fifteen years older than him. Was twenty-five or so years really such a leap? He thought of the sculpture Jack had given him, surely a sign that he recognized the older man's appeal. His heart lightened slightly in his chest. He stopped for a late lunch at Café Flore, where he picked at a chicken Caesar salad and sipped an ice coffee.

Café Whore, they'd always called it and for the last six months, this had been Dwayne's favorite outing. Monkey would bundle him up, a fleece blanket across his lap, his white sneakers angled awkwardly on the footrests, their soles unblemished and laces tied crisply. Monkey would push him the four blocks from the hospice, straining as Market Street tilted up.

"Aren't we the lucky ones?" Dwayne would say as the gym boys passed them on the sidewalk, eyes averted. If the sun was out, they would take a table outside and it was always a damned project to get his wheelchair around the narrow corners. The twenty-somethings were rarely much help and on the worst days it took all of Monkey's restraint not to scream at them. He wanted to get Dwayne settled quickly enough that they could squeeze in thirty or forty minutes before he was once again exhausted. He would help Dwayne with the plastic straw in his chocolate shake. The loud sucking noises, the inevitable dripping onto his sweatshirt. "So, so lucky," Dwayne would say happily as he watched two men lean in for a kiss.

The time since Dwayne's death had passed like an eternity. It had been necessary for him to reinvent his life in so many ways. And now with retirement, he was doing it all over again. When he finished his coffee, Monkey took a cab to the hotel, his leg muscles aching from the combination of his workout and his unplanned trek around the city. Back in his suite, he reviewed an amicus brief for the firm and then went for a short swim and a soak at the hotel's gym. But the hours passed slowly and his stomach fluttered with nerves. He tried to nap, but couldn't and ended up channel surfing restlessly. At ten, he ordered a steak and a bottle of good whiskey from room service. He wished he was at home where he could cook his own damned dinner, drink from his own reserve and be surrounded by the art he and Dwayne had collected.

The contractor had called that afternoon with the news that they'd discovered yet another structural deficit. "Do what you need to," Monkey had said abruptly. He should have booked a trip somewhere, but he'd wanted to stay local to supervise the project. A brilliant idea, clearly. They were already $10,000 over budget. He stopped by every other day and would again the next morning. But they could have been doing anything in there. The job was messy and they were deep in the house's guts. Everything was covered in plastic and coated in a residue of white plaster dust; studs were exposed and whole walls were gone. It struck him as highly unlikely that a few hundred bolts and several carefully-placed pieces of steel could make the difference between the walls caving in on him and staying erect. But the alternative was grimmer to imagine.

When the food arrived, he let the server in with a distracted nod. He stepped out of his room and glanced down the long carpeted hallway in both directions, but it was empty. The server rolled the food cart into the living room, positioning it carefully next to the coffee table. Monkey tipped him with a twenty, which the man pocketed quickly on his way out.

Monkey paced the room. He wasn't actually hungry and he didn't yet feel like a drink. It was already after 10:30. At the large living room window, he peered down at the street. He could make out a crowd piling out of a restaurant, someone walking a dog, a lone figure emerging from a cab and heading into the hotel. The cab pulled away and Monkey's heart beat faster.

Minutes passed and then there was a knock on the door. His stomach jumped. The carpet was soft beneath his bare feet as he approached the door. He took a deep breath, smoothed his hair, and dried his palms on his pants. As he opened the door, he smiled and looked up.

"Your soda water, sir. I'm sorry but we forgot it earlier." The man's English was heavily accented.

Monkey hadn't even noticed the missing water. His heart shrank and he understood that Jack would not be coming, on that night or any other night. The server stepped into the room with the bottle. His uniform was too big by a size and Monkey, who did not bother to check the hall this time, sensed the man's fatigue.

"Would you like to join me?" he asked impulsively. He glanced at the man's chest for a name but the brass tag affixed there simply read W Hotel. "I ordered this for a friend, but he can't join me after all." Monkey gestured towards the untouched steak. The man glanced at his watch.

"Please," Monkey says. "Help yourself. I've already eaten and it'll just go to waste." Monkey studied him. Maybe thirty, his skin a rich brown, sideburns half way down his cheek, a solid gold wedding band. He sat down in the armchair next to the couch. "Thank you," he said.

"Where are you from?" Monkey asked. He poured a whiskey for each of them.

"Argentina. Buenos Aires. I study here, engineering," he said, accepting the tumbler from Monkey.

"Do you miss it?" Monkey uncovered the steak and pushed the cart towards the man. He was talking to keep himself afloat.

"My family, si."

DAMN LOVE

"My name is Douglas," Monkey said.

"Luis." He cut into the steak and took a small bite.

"I know what it's like to be a long way from home."

Luis nodded and took another bite. He chewed rapidly and his hunger was clear.

"Have you seen the view from up here?" Monkey asked.

"Not this room," Luis said.

"I suppose you'd call it the *Extreme Wow* view."

Luis rolled his eyes. Monkey smiled and then crossed the room to the large window. He looked out at the red and white ribbons of headlights bobbing along the Golden Gate Bridge, a vast convoy shuttling people back and forth across the water.

"I study this bridge," Luis said. "I am a seismic engineer. But it is very tough to fix. Seventeen years, they are trying, before the Big One comes. And now, they are, adding a, how do you say," he gestured with his hands. "A web? To catch the people who jump."

"Really? A net?" Monkey said and he thought of people hurling themselves over the bridge and then being caught and bounced into the blue sky like acrobats. If only it was that simple to save someone.

"It is a tricky bridge. But to me it's a puzzle to solve," Luis said.

Monkey nodded. He had wanted to show someone this view, and now he had. Luis tucked into the steak with vigor. Monkey swilled the next sip of whiskey and then he belched before he could stop himself. He winced self-consciously. But Luis didn't look up and instead burped back, the kind of noise that a boy would emit and hold, like a long trumpet note, with great pleasure. They laughed together.

Suddenly Monkey was ravenous. He reached for a handful of fries from Luis' plate and ate them quickly, glad for the salt and crispiness. He reached for more. When they finished the food, Luis stood and left, returning to his shift.

Monkey poured himself another drink and put his feet up on the couch. Time was mostly behind him now, and on that night he could feel it, gusting and propulsive like a wind at his back. From the mantle, the wooden monkey's bright eyes seemed to lock onto his. He thought of Dwayne, staring at him from a tree limb and daring him to leap over the head of an unsuspecting cop; and then he saw Dwayne as he was three weeks from his death, cruising men in the Castro with unmasked pleasure and declaring himself, somehow, the luckiest man alive. For so long, Monkey's heart had cracked open when he thought of those final afternoons. But more and more—if still not entirely—he understood what Dwayne had been trying to say. All along, they'd been counting the wrong things when they tried to measure the good in their lives.

LOVE THE SOLDIER

People see what they want to. As a cop, Keisha counted on that fact, but she also knew it to be true in the off-hours. Take the date she had on Wednesday night. The woman was a lawyer and certifiably hot. But she was also a princess, the type who'd been President of her AKA chapter at Duke and was fond of bringing up the fact that she'd been selected for a Gifted and Talented program at age nine. Every subject that came up—Australian wine, Hurricane Katrina, the incoming class of basketball recruits across the ACC—the lawyer was apparently an expert on. Over dessert, she nibbled on her chocolate torte and asked Keisha whether she actually supported the war or was deploying simply because she had to. The exchange that followed lent a brief spark to the evening, but not enough of one to make Keisha invite her over. That wouldn't have been true even a few months earlier. She'd gone a little crazy after her divorce, but recently, she'd sworn off sleeping with women she didn't want to wake up next to.

"Good policy," her partner Ed said the next morning as they sipped coffee in a white van that was supposed to pass for a contractor's vehicle. They were on Maynard Street, sitting outside a single-story vinyl-sided house with a carport housing a Lexus and a satellite dish in the yard. The house belonged to Fred Monroe, a dealer they'd been playing cat and mouse with for years. His mom actually lived at the address, but he stayed there more often than he did anywhere else. So far, though, there'd been no sign of him.

"So what'd you tell her?" Ed asked.

"I said only a civilian would pose that question."

Ed laughed. At forty, he'd been married for twenty years and had been faithful to his wife except for one truly unfortunate night with a sorority girl in Myrtle Beach in the mid-nineties. He rubbed the stubble on his cheeks, red like his hair. He was sunburned from a weekend of jet skiing at Jordan Lake. *Could you be any whiter if you tried?* Keisha had asked when he showed up for work that Monday as pink as a roasted pig, his neck and forearms looking like bubble wrap from all the blisters.

The house's front door opened. A woman in a floral house-dress and fluffy purple slippers emerged on the stoop. She walked down three concrete steps and retrieved the morning paper from the sidewalk. She peered at the van for a moment and then shook her head.

"Mama needs some coffee," Keisha said. "And a new land-scaper." A wishing well with a shingled roof sat on the fresh-ly-mowed lawn. A smiling gnome with a chipped arm leaned against it.

"My mother-in-law gave us one just like that we bought our first house. I had to put the goddamn thing up every time she came to visit," Ed said.

Keisha laughed. She'd met his mother-in-law at one of Ed's son's birthday parties. They'd been close like that since Marcus' death in 2001. Marcus was Keisha's older brother and had been Ed's best friend in the Durham PD. From the time Keisha enrolled at the Academy, less than a year after Marcus was murdered by another cop, Ed had kept an eye on her. They'd been partners for the past two years.

On Monday morning, Keisha's National Guard Unit would head to Fort Pendleton for three weeks of training and then ship out to Fallujah. Her mother was calling twice a day to go over the weekend's plans: the Yellow Ribbon Ceremony in Raleigh on Saturday; a lunch for friends and family after church on Sunday; driving her down to Fort Bragg first thing Monday morning, where she'd meet up with her unit. The send off was as thoroughly planned as Keisha's wedding had been six years earlier.

Her father was the Senior Pastor at one of the larger Baptist churches in Durham. His response to her deployment had been to hold a press conference about the disproportionate effects of the war on communities of color. Press conference or not, though, she was shipping out and her job was simple. She needed to make sure everyone in her unit came back alive. Back when she was being recruited by top basketball programs, her father had used it as an occasion to decry the NCAA as a modern day auction block. But for the four years she played shooting guard at Carolina, he was at every home game and traveled with the team whenever he could, decked out in a Tarheel shirt that bore her number. She adored him, but he was a peacock. She was furious with him and she forgave him. All of it true at once.

It was easy to let her mind wander on stake-outs. The radio hissed. Ed crushed a Krispy Kreme bag into a ball, tossed it into the back of the van and licked the glaze from his thumb and forefinger. A chubby white kid on a cheap mountain bike weaved up the sidewalk and back down, his mouth stained cherry red.

Lights were on in the house, but no one was coming or going. Fred Monroe's crew had its hands in a shipment of heroin that was making its way up the 95 corridor in the next seventy-two hours. They were on his ass day and night. But Monroe was disciplined, all about calculated risks. So they waited and watched.

Keisha and Ed had arrested him twice in the last year and he always lawyered up immediately. His mother had a stash of cash tucked away and instructions to call his lawyer any time of day or night. The lawyer, also named Monroe, was a bloated blonde who wore seersucker and bow ties without a trace of irony. *Only in North Cackalacky*, Ed had said when they'd first realized that the men were distant cousins.

On the job, there were two simple rules: Always know where you are and where your partner is. Everything else was a mess and, Keisha had learned, odds were good that your first impression of what exactly was happening at a domestic disturbance or a crime scene would be inaccurate. She'd trust her life to Fred Monroe sooner than she would his lawyer. She'd arrested a pediatrician on molestation charges, executing a warrant on his beach house and finally turning up a stash of kiddie porn in his wine cellar. She'd booked a man she knew to be innocent on murder charges. She'd been the first on the scene of three births, five suicides, and one familicide. Everyone—every last soul she knew—was just one or two moves away from committing a crime. *We've all got some dirt in our backyards*, Ed liked to say.

Growing up a preacher's kid had been decent training for the job: a knock on the door at 2 AM, a deacon, who also happened to be a State Senator, and his wife on the porch in a driving rain. Her father escorting them into his office, her mother putting on coffee. Keisha and Marcus watched from the top of the carpeted stairs, retreating quickly when an adult walked through the living room. Hushed voices, the deacon's wife's crying, and then the next morning an article in the paper about corruption charges and a FBI investigation. That Sunday, the couple sat in the front row as special guests of her father's and months later, the deacon started a one-year federal prison sentence. Her father visited him regularly. Circle the wagons when trouble hits; innocent until proven guilty, no matter what the evidence looks like. Sins were forgiven, overlooked or buried deep in the ground.

An unremarkable six hours later, their shift on Maynard Street was over. Monroe hadn't budged from the house, if he was there at all. "He would've spotted us a mile away," Keisha said as Ed pulled away from the curb. Some genius in the police garage had affixed ad magnets for a fake painting company to both sides of the van and had tied a paint-spattered ladder onto the roof with bungee cords. But for anyone who expected to be trailed, the effect would be unconvincing.

At headquarters, Keisha emptied the contents of her locker into a duffel bag. Her official leave began in one day. She would be leaving behind five active investigations and a handful more that were headed to trial. It was Monroe who bothered her, though. She'd pulled a handful of double shifts in the last few weeks to push the case along and there'd been some progress. They'd picked up one of his lieutenants on a probation violation and an informant had told them about this shipment. But Narcotics cases had to be built slowly, and even then they were still a house of cards.

Keisha went home to finish packing. Her to-do list was on the fridge, a line through the completed items. Her downtown condo was rented, furnished, to a grad student from NC Central. Her parents were taking LeRoy, a boxer mix with a bad under bite that her ex, James, had trained to fetch the remote. Since she'd started packing, LeRoy had been following her around the condo, watching every movement and when she put on her shoes, racing to the door and grabbing his leash in his mouth.

She'd be away for eighteen months. As a MP, she'd be patrolling Camp Freedom, the largest base in Fallujah, as they shut it down. She'd also be training members of the Iraqi Defense Forces to take over once the withdrawal was complete. *Can't you request office duty?* her mother had asked. She still didn't understand that Keisha had enlisted because she wanted to serve.

Other than the furniture, all that was left in the apartment were the few dishes she'd need for the weekend, her toiletry kit, her Bible, laptop, phone, and the clothes she'd take with her. LeRoy hopped into the front seat as she loaded the last boxes of books and clothes into the back of her truck. He would be spending the weekend with her parents to make sure he settled in before she left. Her father snuck LeRoy raw hot dogs and bites of ice cream and she knew he'd be obese by the time she got home. It embarrassed her that she teared up whenever she thought about saying goodbye to him.

Just three miles away, her parents' house was empty when she arrived. An oversized glass bowl filled with granny smith apples sat on butcher block island, part of her mother's grand plan to reduce her father by fifty pounds. "You're killing me," he would moan when she served him grilled tilapia and steamed broccoli.

LeRoy close on her heels, Keisha dragged the boxes down to the finished basement and piled them on top of the dusty, scratched pool table that she and Marcus had destroyed in high school. A glass case displayed the bulk of her trophies. The national championship trophy, they kept in the family room. Back upstairs, she walked down the first floor hall toward the bathroom, her eyes lingering on the framed family photos that lined the wall. She was relieved to see that her mom had finally taken down the family portrait from her wedding day.

In its place was a black and white photo of her parents from Freedom Summer, where they'd met. They looked heartbreakingly young, but also ready for the world, sipping Cokes in the backseat of a black Ford Fairlane, returning from a weekend of registering voters in McComb, Mississippi. Each night, her father had walked her mother to the girls dorm at the small black college the volunteers were staying at in Jackson. And late in the summer, after they were engaged, Keisha's mother had nursed her father through a broken rib and collarbone when he was jumped by a group of Ole Miss football players barhopping down in Jackson.

Keisha had heard those stories her entire life, burned into her like the gospels had been on Sundays, or the Greek myths her English teacher had made them memorize in 7th grade. Hercules, Eurydice, Paul, Matthew, Fannie Lou Hamer, John Lewis, the names and stories had bled together in her twelve-year old mind and in each of them she had heard different versions of the same message: you have inherited a great and mighty debt, and it will take all you've got—blood, sweat, tears, love, duty, life itself—to pay it off. She knew how much had been sacrificed on her behalf, and this knowledge was with her even as she slept. She might shy from the political frays and social causes that were her parents' lifeblood, but it did not mean she lived without a code.

All the photos taken before 2001 included Marcus. Four years older than she was, he'd been a cop until he'd been shot when he was off-duty. Another cop had pulled the trigger, a veteran who spotted Marcus circling the back of a house on Maynard, not far from where Monroe lived. Keisha had spent hundreds of hours reading and rereading the case file, the IRB reports, and the autopsy. She could see it all: Someone had called in a report of an armed robbery in progress. The veteran had been first on the scene. Poor visibility in the rainy dark. His feet crunching the gravel driveway. The house, an unremarkable brick rancher, storm door hanging from a loose hinge, all the windows darkened. "I saw a figure come around the back," the cop said, "and he clearly had a weapon drawn. I ordered him to put the weapon down three times. He was non-compliant." That's how the story went. There was no concrete evidence of foul play. Even her father eventually told her to drop it.

Keisha still wore Marcus' cross and fingered it reflexively when she saw his broad, grinning face in photos. His death had changed everything. She'd graduated from Carolina in '97 and played pro in the WNBA for four years, first for New York and then for Phoenix. She'd torn her ACL heading into the 2001 play offs. A week later, Marcus had been shot, and then 9/11 had happened. In the utter, brutal mess of that time, her father had led rallies outside the Mayor's office for two weeks after Marcus' death, demanding that the cop who shot him get fired. Ultimately, he'd gotten suspended for three weeks and then reinstated to the force, where he'd headed up a short-lived Counter Terrorism Unit that occupied itself monitoring the two mosques in Durham.

Everyone whom she usually listened to counseled Keisha to take a few months off before making any decisions. But she knew what she needed to do. She opted out of her contract renewal with Phoenix, moved home, finished rehabbing her knee, applied to the academy and started dating James. She had walked away from at least another five years of playing, and from a life in which she could do what she wanted, date who she wanted. In New York and Phoenix, she was anonymous. But between her father's church and her reputation as a local kid made good, she was under a microscope back in Durham.

It was all worth it, though. She knew her revenge would come in the form of being an exemplary cop. Every time that asshole saw her in uniform, he'd be reminded of what he'd done, and every case she closed, every promotion she earned, would be for Marcus.

**

On Friday morning, she and Ed followed Monroe to the Washington Duke Golf Course, where they inched along the property line in an unmarked Ford. Through binoculars, they watched him play nine holes with his lawyer. "He should be ashamed to be seen in those things," Keisha said of the lawyer's pants, butter yellow and spotted with ducks. Fred was dressed like Tiger in a red dry fit shirt and black pants. But the similarities ended there.

"This is excruciating," Ed said as they watched Fred whiff a drive and then immediately hack at the ball again, sending it a jerky forty yards down the green.

"You think they teach golf in juvie?" Keisha laughed. But the men weren't there to play. The golf course, steamy and nearly empty, afforded them the privacy they were looking for.

There was nothing Keisha and Ed could do but watch, wait and follow Fred to his next destination. The likelihood that they'd turn up anything was slim, but their boss liked to keep pressure on when big shipments were moving. Even if they came up with grounds to question Monroe and if he revealed anything worth knowing, it wouldn't stop the shipment. They all knew that and yet they stayed in motion.

The first time they'd arrested him it had been for shooting another dealer in the face at point-blank range. She and Ed happened to be a block over and were on-scene in less than a minute, but Fred had already gotten rid of the gun. She'd had to choke down her own vomit at the sight of grey matter on the sidewalk, but Fred's eyes had been clear, his affect unchanged, as she slapped on the cuffs and the approaching ambulance siren wailed. His lawyer had met them at the police station and Fred was out on bail before the sun came up. The case never went to trial: there was no gun, there were no witnesses, and he had no gunpowder residue on his fingers.

The day progressed, and they trailed Monroe to a boxing gym for a sparring session, to his ex-wife's house, and then to Best Buy, where he bought a flat screen TV. Civilians tended to think that cons spent every second of the day plotting their next illicit activity. But the sad truth was that most stakeouts were like watching a boring reality show. This one was different only because it would be her last shift with Ed. By the time she returned from her tour, he would have settled in with a new partner and she'd be shuffled back into the rotation.

Ed had known about Keisha since her divorce. *Look*, he said when she told him. *We're family. Who cares who you sleep with?* She appreciated the sentiment. But the truth was that a lot of people would care, starting with her parents, her church, her commanding officer in the National Guard, and the Police Chief. Take all that away and what would be left?

The badge, the uniform, the battered metal locker, target practice, fitness tests: it all suited her. Other things, like marriage to James, had not. She'd known that, but she had still said yes, determined to make it work, the same way she'd learned to dribble and shoot with her left hand, or had made it through a playoff game with a broken foot in her first season with New York. If she failed James in some essential ways, she tried to make up for it in others. She never objected to his boys' nights out and she never said no to sex, although she often had to will her way through it, his lips rubbery on hers, his touch probing rather than welcome. She had tried to love him the way he needed her to. But it was like asking a dog to start talking.

When their shift ended, Keisha turned in her badge, her gun, her uniform and her belt. Ed waited out in the hall and then walked her to her truck. He'd be at the lunch on Sunday, along with most of the department, but he handed her a wrinkled paper bag from Food Lion. "Wait 'til you get home," he said and then hugged her. His 5'o'clock shadow scratched her forehead and she could smell the familiar combination of his sweat and deodorant.

"I'm going to miss you," he said.

"Mr. Feelings!" Keisha said, making a puppet with her index finger. His wife had been dragging Ed to counseling for the past year and the therapist had been making Ed express his emotions with a finger puppet by this name.

Ed gave Keisha the finger. "Fuck you."

"Did you download Skype like I told you?" she asked, opening the door and sliding behind the wheel.

He nodded. She could feel her throat tightening, but didn't want to cry. "I'll see you Sunday," she said.

At her kitchen table, she drank a bottle of Bud Light and opened the paper bag, pulling out a framed picture of Ed and Marcus. They were in police grays, their arms around each other. They must have just finished a training run. Dark sweat stains covered Marcus' chest and beads of sweat ran down his forehead. He looked so alive in the photo, as if she could touch his chest and feel his heart beating. She slipped the back of the frame off and turned the print over. In blue ink, Ed had scrawled, his handwriting still like a boy's, *Timed 5K. First place, Marcus Caldwell, 17:02.* Under that he'd written, *To: Keisha. Stay Safe. Love, Ed.*

She slipped the photo into an envelope in her Bible, along with ones of her parents, LeRoy, James, Alex, and one of Marcus and her. In it, they were standing below the hoop their dad had installed in the driveway; Marcus was fourteen, she was ten. He'd beaten her twenty-one to eight and she'd stormed off the court. He'd finally coaxed her into a rematch, which he'd won twenty-one to four. She'd hated him that day, but he'd known what he was doing. He taught her how to play.

Her condo felt like a sterile model home and she missed LeRoy's moping around, watching TV with her. An email arrived from the lawyer and she was surprised to find that it made her smile. *I'm around this weekend if you'd like to get a drink before leaving town.* Despite the date, Keisha had thought about the woman several times since then, her easy, warm laugh, her green eyes, the smooth confidence with which she paid the bill. As Friday night ticked past, it was tempting to call her. But she didn't and instead replied by email, friendly but short, the kind that would invite a response.

**

She'd invited only her parents to the Yellow Ribbon Ceremony, which was held in a high school auditorium in Raleigh. The rest of her unit was there, all men, mostly cops and state troopers, a few teachers and engineers. Alex had offered to fly in from San Francisco for the weekend. But she cringed at the idea of Alex's spending all that time with her parents. She just didn't have it in her to go there. The issue had never come up with her parents. Not once in her thirty-five years. During coffee hour after church, women were always trying to set her up with their single sons, half of whom Keisha knew from the gay bars around town. Her mother would demure on her behalf. "She's still not ready," as if the divorce had inflicted a deep wound.

But as the day and the ceremony unfolded, Keisha missed Alex. They'd known each other since they were six and Alex was the first woman she'd ever kissed. She was a doctor out in San Francisco and Keisha had been out to see her the month before. She could see imagine her there with them, in a well-cut suit, probably wearing lipstick and earrings to tone the gay vibe down a few notches. She would have been taking hundreds of pictures and getting water for Keisha's mother, talking politics and sports with her father.

Alex had been at everything that mattered. Back in college, she'd flown down to New Orleans for the National Championship game and she'd later made the trip to New York for Keisha's

WNBA debut. In 2001, she'd been there for the entire hellish week after Marcus got shot.

Alex had been in med school at Carolina and had ditched class and driven straight to the ER at Duke, where the waiting room was already packed with cops and half the church. Keisha's parents were given a small room for privacy and Alex had come and gone from there, acting as an interpreter between the family and the harried trauma surgeon, who seemed unable to communicate in anything but medical terminology. It had been Alex who first thought to monitor Keisha's father's blood pressure and had thus saved them a second admission to the ER that day.

Late that night, Alex had picked Keisha up from the airport. They'd ridden back to the hospital in silence, but as they pulled into the parking garage, Alex had told her that someone needed to talk to the doctors about life support. Marcus was in the ICU by then, but he was brain dead. The first bullet had pierced his left lung, the second one had gone in through his forehead. One millimeter to the left and it would have killed him instantly. It was a nightmare.

For all these years, their whole lives almost, she and Alex had been circling each other. During college, Keisha had watched as Alex came out and brought home a string of skinny, whiny girlfriends who wrote poetry and had weird dietary restrictions. Then Keisha had gotten drafted and left North Carolina, just as Alex moved home to start med school. By the time Keisha retired, Alex was already with Emily, whom Keisha actually liked, with her tattoos and bright lipstick and husky voice. Alex had moved to San Francisco for her residency, but she had flown back home for Keisha's wedding, going through all the motions at her bachelorette party, handing out programs, looking awkward in a dress. It was only in the last six months that they'd both been single at the same time. But even now, they were 3,000 miles apart and Keisha was about to double that distance.

"Compartmentalize much?" Alex had said in a rare dark moment between them, on the night that Keisha had told her she was marrying James. "How can you do this to yourself?" But for Keisha there were bigger truths, more urgent ones. Her parents needed her, and she them. Nothing mattered more and it was that simple. White people were fucked up in that way: obsessed with things that didn't matter, like the label you hung over your bed, and cavalier about things that did, like actually seeing your parents more than once a year, the way Alex was content to.

The problem was that Alex wanted everything to be easy, even love. In San Francisco, she lived in her own orbit. Out there, duty was nothing more than an abstraction, and a dull one at that. Not to say that it wasn't fun. When Keisha had visited, they'd gone dancing on Thursday night and on Friday, there'd been an afternoon picnic at Ocean Beach—fresh baked bread, smoked cheese, strawberries, chocolate, red wine. The wind was blowing but the fog hadn't rolled in yet. It was warm enough to take off your sweatshirt and roll up your jeans. A pack of school kids, maybe eight or nine, was roaming the beach, bending over every few seconds to poke at potential specimens, collecting shells and pieces of seaweed in clear plastic bags.

Alex leaned in to kiss her, but Keisha's body went rigid and she pulled back. It was pure reflex: her stomach contracted to a fist, her shoulder blades clenched, her eyes tracked the kids on the beach, their clipboard-holding teacher. She felt exposed and indecent and she waited for the teacher to hustle her students away from them. Alex, still leaning in, stared at her, and then turned away and clenched her jaw. Keisha reached for a strawberry and ate it, unrolled her jeans, stared at the ocean. For awhile, they didn't talk. Hours later, walking to dinner in the Castro, Keisha had reached for Alex's hand, trying to close the distance that had opened up between them.

**

On Sunday morning, Keisha picked her mother up for church at 9:30. Her father had left the house at six to finish his sermon and primp. "Your dog did his business on your father's shoes," her mother reported as she pulled herself into the passenger seat. She was wearing a new yellow suit with a matching purse and heels. Keisha was in an A-line black skirt and blazer.

The church's front doors were thrown open and sunlight streamed in. A middle-aged woman stood at the welcome table with a basket full of yellow ribbons, handing them out along with programs. She smiled at Keisha like she thought it would make the difference between her living and dying. Keisha tried not to cringe. Then again, the whole service, which her father was dedicating to all the active-duty soldiers and veterans in the congregation, made her feel that way. The church had lost a nineteen-year-old to a car bombing in Mosul and had two guys currently serving in the same unit in Baghdad. But she didn't trust her father to get it right or to respect the central premise of a deployment: you plan to come home alive.

Her mother worked the crowd. She smiled and waved at key committee chairs, walked chillily past the woman her husband had slept with twenty years earlier. She sought out the mother of the dead nineteen-year-old, wrapping her in a warm hug. As the organist hit the first chord of the anthem, an usher in a black suit and white gloves escorted them to the front row, where they were on display.

An hour into the service, her father began his sermon. He wiped his forehead with a white handkerchief and scanned the congregation, letting a silence settle over them. "How many times now have you heard me say I oppose this war?" The congregation murmured. Next to her, Keisha's mother adjusted herself. The nurses in the front three rows glanced over at them.

"I want to talk to you today about Abraham and Isaac. We've been over this text before, but never under these circumstances. Never when God is saying to me, to us, *turn your child over to the world's troubles. Stand there and watch as she treads right into the bowels of hell.*

There were over 1,000 people in the sanctuary. Even with the air conditioning on, the room was hot. Woman waved cardboard fans emblazoned with the church's logo and a painting of Jesus on the cross. It was on that altar that she'd been confirmed and baptized and years later, had taken her vows to James. It was on that altar that Marcus' closed steel casket had laid during the funeral. Her father might think war was hell, but for her nothing could be as desolate, as excruciating as the moment in which she'd nodded to the doctor because her parents were simply unable to do so. The machines unplugged, they'd stood around Marcus' bed, holding his hands, their mother stroking his face whispering, *sweet baby, sweet baby* into his ear. Four minutes later, he was gone.

"Now let me be clear," he went on. "I am *not* saying that I am Abraham, or that my daughter is Isaac. But you see, I'm confused, and it's not because I don't know my Hebrew Scriptures or my theology. It's because God is asking more of me than I am prepared to do and I'm looking for anything I can grab onto to keep from plummeting into the abyss."

People murmured more loudly. This is why they loved him. Why he was the one they called when babies were born, when the police knocked on the door. Why women and men alike felt like, in his arms, they could cry. He had baptized a third of the congregation, married at least that many, buried the loved ones of most of them. He had heard their secrets and when they called, he came.

But for three months after Marcus died, he hadn't been able to preach. She'd moved home to be with her parents, where she recovered from knee surgery and slept in her childhood bedroom. For those first few weeks, she and her parents were like ghosts in the house, remembering to eat only because two women from the church would arrive with a steaming hot meal and set the table for them. Each day, her mother accompanied her to her physical therapy appointments as she rehabbed her knee, and at night they watched movies and bad sit coms together. Anything to pass the time.

Saturday nights, Keisha would wake up in the middle of the night and she'd hear music coming from his study. Coltrane, Davis, Aretha. Sometimes, she'd go downstairs and find him at his desk in his robe and slippers, his leather bound Bible in front of him but shut.

"God's left me," he told her on one of those nights, shaking his head, his voice cracking. "If it weren't for your mother," he said, his voice trailing off.

"I know," she'd said, and she'd sat down on the couch in his office, pulling a blanket over her legs. He'd pour her a tumbler of whiskey and they'd stay like that, talking about Marcus as if their stories could somehow resurrect him. When the sun finally came up, she'd put on a pot of coffee and her father would go upstairs to shower and hours later, they'd leave for church, where he would preside over the service, but turn the pulpit over to his Associate Minister when the time came for the sermon. Then, he would walk down and sit with his wife in the front pew, holding her hand, his head bowed.

Sitting in that same pew these years later, she watched her father. He wore a goatee these days and his dark face showed hardly any wrinkles. He could pass for a 45-year-old, and carried himself like the linebacker he'd been back in high school. He'd grown up Harlem, raised by a single mother who worked three jobs to put him through Rutgers. He went down to Mississippi during Freedom Summer as a Plan B because a summer internship had fallen through and from there things had moved quickly: meeting her mother, applying to seminary, getting his first church. *The world is yours*, he had told Keisha and Marcus over and over again when they were growing up. *We risked everything so that the world could be yours.*

"Today, I am not just your preacher," he went on. "I am not just President of the Southern Association. I am not just the man you see on the news. Today, I am also a flawed, broken man. I am Robert Caldwell. Loving husband of Michelle Caldwell. Devoted father of Marcus and Keisha Caldwell. My son was killed nine years ago and it left me a broken man. The way some of you have been broken. I know you hear me when I say that I would give my own life to have him back here." He paused.

"All I would ask is that we might pass each as we traveled between the lands of the living and the dead, that I might lay eyes on him for just one more moment. But God's not answering that prayer." He picked the pace up. "Instead, my baby girl is going to fight a war I despise and I am terrified. This is the naked truth, brothers and sisters. So I go to Scripture, and I say, Lord, show me the way here, because I am lost. I say, Father, how far are you going to push me this time? Are you going to push me as far as you pushed Abraham?"

His voice dropped to a whisper. "You've got to show me the way here, Lord." His eyes scanned the congregation and he let the silence grow. He was, Keisha knew, getting ready for the pivot point, for the long climb back out, and as he resumed speaking, his voice rose again. "Show me the way, Lord. Show me the way," he thundered.

Her mother reached over and took her hand, her skin cool and dry as her fingers enveloped Keisha's. Her father's sermon lasted another ten minutes, and ultimately, he came out where he tended to: He would love the soldier but hate the war. Same as he loved the sinner but hated the sin.

That night, Keisha drove to Mirage, a gay bar in Raleigh. She was exhausted from the weekend—the Yellow Ribbon ceremony, the church service, the catered luncheon at her parents' house that seventy-five people had come to. All she wanted was to sit at the bar, drink a few gin and tonics, and shoot the shit with Nick, who'd be bartending. She'd always liked Sunday nights, people mellowing out, the regulars filtering in and out, sports on the TV, the place quiet.

"Are you ready?" Nick said. He managed the club and on a handful of occasions, Keisha had helped him out of tough spots.

"All I do is head to New Jersey tomorrow," she said, smiling. She slid her credit card across the bar.

But he shook his head and pushed the card back. "It's on us tonight."

She was one of maybe twenty people there, but she didn't pay any attention to the other customers. Even a few months ago, she would have been restless, cruising the room, turning around anytime someone knew walked in, often enough going home with someone she wouldn't have looked at twice in the light of day. This was where she'd met the lawyer a few weeks earlier. The women had walked in with a group of friend, wearing tight jeans, heels and a sleeveless black shirt. A martini in one hand, she'd been the one to approach Keisha. This weekend, they'd sent a few emails back and forth. Maybe it meant something, maybe not.

"I've loved you for as long as I can remember," Alex had said as they laid in bed when Keisha was out in San Francisco.

"I know," Keisha had said, reaching for her, kissing her breasts, her stomach, her thighs. This memory, she would carry with her. What came next between them, there was no way to know. Eighteen months was a long time: enough time for a war to end; for she or Alex to fall in love with someone else; for her father to lose fifty pounds or have a heart attack; for her mother to go through her boxes and find the letters and pictures and figure it all out, or not. It was all too much to think about. She needed things to stay simple.

She watched the Braves game on the TV over the bar and sipped her drink.

"You've got an admirer," Nick said. He poured her a fresh gin and tonic, nodding towards the pool table.

Keisha turned around. From across the room, she saw Fred Monroe. He was wearing baggy jeans, a black button down and a black Kangol cap, which he tipped in her direction.

She'd made it her business to know everything about Monroe, but this was news to her. He was with a drag queen whom Keisha recognized from the club. She performed as Ms. Beyond C-Cup. She was thin, with long legs, a tight stomach, full lips. Unlike many of the queens who performed at the club—campy, overweight men who dressed as Cher or Carolina cheerleaders—she was convincing in all the right ways. A few months earlier, it had amused Keisha to realize that she was turned on as she'd watch Ms. Beyond C-Cup straddle a chair in fishnet hose during a show.

Fred walked towards her with drink in hand. Ms. Beyond C-Cup sipped on a cocktail and perched on the edge of the pool table.

"I hear you shipping out," Fred said. "My cuz is over there. Baghdad." He sat on the stool next to Keisha.

She nodded. The last time she'd been this close to him, she was booking him, shoving him into the back of her squad car.

But with her badge inactive, she had no power over him anymore. She took a sip of the drink he'd bought her and sucked on a piece of ice. "Thanks," she said.

"You know, Keisha, you and me, it's like we're on opposite sides of this fence. You can see through it, and you can climb over or under it, but it goes on forever." He paused and took a swallow of whiskey. "I always liked you, though."

She glanced at his eyes. He was stoned but in control. "You having fun with your friend?" she asked.

"She's high maintenance," he said, grinning in a slow, satisfied way.

"I'm sure she is," Keisha said, laughing despite herself.

"When you're back, we should talk."

Keisha didn't say anything.

Monroe looked away and then put his drink down on the bar. "I was there the night your brother went down."

Her whole body stiffened.

"That's some sorry ass cover up job they did."

"The investigation is closed," Keisha said. She had dissected those reports. But as much as she'd wanted to, she'd found nothing out of the ordinary in the reams of paper.

"You mean the one that said he was off-duty instead of undercover for the feds? Or that failed to mention that your pussy ass partner was on scene?"

"What are you talking about, Fred?" Keisha got in his face. She could smell the whiskey on his breath, the cologne on his neck.

He put his hands up and laughed. "I like it when you get hot."

He stepped away and then paused. "I almost forgot. My mom, she saw your dad on the news and now get this, she's got a crush on him. She's been nagging the hell out of me and I promised to take her to church next Sunday. So, here's the thing. Should I tell people I know you professionally?" He paused and gestured around the club. "Or socially?"

He smiled and then returned to the pool table. Ms. Beyond C-Cup draped herself over him, whispering into his ear. His laughter carried across the bar.

Keisha drained her drink. "I'll see you, Nick," she called out, leaving a twenty on the bar. She headed out through the rear exit and toward her truck in the back of the lot, where it faced away from the street.

Shake it off, she told herself, instructing her body as if it was a machine. Cons specialized in head games, and for all she knew, Monroe had followed her there and paid the drag queen to spend an hour with him. But regardless, Fred had done what he intended to: the seed of doubt was planted. The story of that night—always a little too neat, but documented in such a way that she couldn't find the weak spots—blossomed again in her mind. And she knew that it would be her constant companion for the next eighteen months: patrol duty, a cold, starless desert night, a caravan of Humvees rolling in, and this was what she'd be thinking about. Fred was lying, or not, but either way, this would torture her, and he knew it.

She pulled into the street and headed towards her condo, where she'd sleep on the couch, her packed bags lined up by the front door. She thought about the day that had just passed. How Ed had choked up as he made a toast at the luncheon. How her father had done the same.

Abraham and Isaac, he'd told the congregation that morning, and they'd walked down that path with him, seeing her as the wide-eyed youngest child, her skinny body laid out on the altar, her fate in her father's trembling hands, intervening angels rushing in, God having a good cosmic chuckle. But he'd gotten it wrong. If she was anyone at all in that story, it was Ishmael: the chameleon whose story everyone told differently, casting him as bastard, prophet, warrior. Ishmael, the desert-bound outcast, destined to live 137 years.

It was midnight when she got home. She brushed her teeth and washed her face. In six hours, she would pull into her parent's driveway and let herself into the kitchen. LeRoy would greet her eagerly, her father would be running late and her mother would be overdressed. The sky would still be dark as they pulled onto I-40 and later 95 in her father's car. Her mother would be contradicting the GPS, her father talking back to Tom Joyner as if the man could hear him, and LeRoy would be drooling on her lap in the backseat. They'd stop at McDonalds for coffee and biscuits on the outskirts of Fayetteville. They'd glide through security at Fort Bragg and park. For a moment, they'd sit silently in the car and then Keisha would start to speak and she would find some way to tell her parents that it would all be ok, that their hearts would not be broken a second time. Her own heart was another matter, best tended to in private. She'd built everything upon that premise. Never mind the risk, she'd always told herself, as if her life was nothing more than another tournament to be played, another battle to be fought.

She slept on her couch. At 5:30, she woke up before her alarm and dressed quickly in uniform. She grabbed her bags, locked the door behind her, and walked to her truck. Morning dew covered the grass and her windshield. The sun was rising. The sky was silver and pink. A hawk circled above her. These things were simple and beautiful. They should have brought her solace, but they did not.

LAYOVER

It took three days, but Carlos finally returned Brenda's call. She listened to his message as she deplaned from a red eye on Christmas morning, emerging from the stale air of the plane into a pre-dawn Reagan National. Even recorded, Carlos' voice made her stomach, already churning from morning sickness, jump. But calling him back wasn't an option: 6 AM in DC meant 3 AM in San Francisco, where he'd still be tangled in the sheets with Cassie, his ex-wife-now-girlfriend. Two weeks ago, he'd broken up with Brenda and moved back in with Cassie.

Passing still-darkened stores and groggy travelers trying to reassemble themselves post-security check, Brenda walked to her connecting gate. There, she chose a chair facing a bank of windows, her hips squeezing against the arm rests on the plastic chair and reminding her, as countless things did, of the thirty pounds she needed to lose. Outside, heavy snow fell, flakes pocking the dawn sky and layering the grey tarmac. The storm had already shuttered airports in Boston, New York and Philadelphia.

"Please be advised that the 6:45 flight to Atlanta has been delayed, with an estimated departure time of 11:00," a woman's voice announced over the loudspeaker in a neutral tone.

The man next to Brenda, unshaven and wearing a Jets jersey, groaned. "I spent twenty-four hours at Newark while these idiots cancelled three flights. So I finally take a cab down here and now look at this. My daughter's getting married in twelve hours in Florida."

Brenda murmured vaguely, the way she did with intractable patients when she was tired. She pulled a diet energy bar from the mess of her purse and grimaced at the first chalky bite. If nothing else, her breakup with Carlos had made her wildly productive and for once, work deadlines weren't looming. Her patient charts were up to date, she'd proofed two articles and written evaluations of the students she'd supervised that fall. Brenda usually volunteered to be on call over Christmas. Last year that had involved getting a sixteen-year-old admitted to a psych hospital for suicide watch and fielding calls from patients for whom the forced cheer of the season was excruciating.

Under the terminal's high ceiling, she felt invisible and unencumbered. She wasn't exactly in a rush to get to Atlanta, where she would be spending Christmas Day with her father's family. Months ago, her grandmother had sent her a message on Facebook with the assistance of a home health aide who had also helped her set up an online dating profile. Brenda's last memory of her grandmother was from her father's funeral. But that suddenly, three decades of silence ended.

Phone calls had followed and with them came revelations about the birthday cards and checks that her grandmother had sent her throughout childhood and that, apparently, Brenda's mom had intercepted. Then, this invitation to the annual Davis Family Christmas Party, which would include dozens of distant cousins, a cakewalk, and a white elephant gift exchange. Imagining all that small talk—the impossibility of making up for thirty years of absence, explaining again and again that no, there was no husband, or fiancée, no, not even a boyfriend—Brenda had delayed making a decision. But her grandmother was a tireless suitor and Brenda finally booked a trip that had her arriving in time for Christmas lunch and staying at a Marietta hotel for just two nights.

In the past month, the potentially disastrous reunion had come to seem like a welcome relief from the actual mess of her life. She and Carlos had been together five months and she'd been on the verge of telling him she was in love with him and —*oops!*—pregnant. But then he'd opted not to stay at her house for two nights and stopped answering her calls on the first ring. He'd asked her out for a drink at a restaurant that was always crowded and had greeted her at the bar with a hug but no kiss. His eyes locked on his beer, he'd explained that his ex-wife had asked him to move back in. Brenda had nodded, taken a cab home, and spent four hours reorganizing her bookshelves, the worker bees of disassociation already laying miles of track between her and Carlos.

He called ten times that night and six times the next day, but she'd waited two weeks to call him back. This latest message was his response. The next move was hers. On her calendar Brenda had marked the last date she could get an abortion with a small black X. She had gone as far as scheduling an appointment at a clinic. But each passing day felt like the click of a gun barrel. She wanted to stop time just long enough to catch her breath, to somehow discern which choice she wouldn't come to regret. She'd told only one person, her best friend, Kathryn.

The overhead speaker crackled again. "Please be advised that Flight 2359 to Atlanta has been delayed until 3 PM." The man next to her buried his head in his hands. "What the hell am I supposed to tell my daughter? She's marrying her high school boyfriend before he ships out to basic training. I said, wait till his leave this summer and we'll do at the Shore, but she already had her heart set on a winter beach wedding. Everyone flew down to Naples two days ago, but I had to pull one more shift."

"What do you do?" Brenda asked.

"I'm a cop, New Brunswick Police Department. Steve." He

reached out his hand and she shook it.

"Brenda," she offered.

He nodded and craned his neck toward the line of passengers forming at the ticket counter. "This is gonna be a total clusterfuck."

Tinny Christmas carols flowed from the airport's sound system. Brenda watched the human flow moving restlessly from food court to gate to bathroom to bookstore. A baby-faced soldier in fatigues and thick glasses slept on the floor using his duffel bag as a pillow. A toddler raced back and forth in front of him, his mother watching over crossed, weary arms.

The situation with Carlos was constantly on her mind, like a radio station she couldn't turn off. Even in the midst of counseling sessions with clients, she was thinking about it. It bothered her that she'd met Carlos at a wedding and bothered her even more that she'd noticed him immediately—his dark hair cut short, his warm eyes, his aquiline nose, the inviting contrast of his blue shirt and brown skin. His elbow on the bar, he'd leaned close when he asked for her number. Drunk, she'd actually written it on the back of his hand, as if they were seventeen. He'd called the next day. On their first date, he'd mentioned his divorce but she'd been unconcerned and had steered the conversation back to sci fi movies. She was looking for company, not a husband.

They went on a second and then a third date, and then a few weeks later, she found herself watching him sleep, running a finger down his jaw line, her other hand on the tuft of black hair on his sternum. She felt her heart's turning towards him and imagined it like a satellite in the sky, training its lens on a new star.

"Don't treat your lovers like clients," Kathryn had warned her again and again over the years, and though Brenda cringed at the word lover, she knew her friend was right. People always told her their secrets too easily, too quickly, and whether they realized it or not, the exchange was almost always transactional: Brenda was willing to hold their stories as long as she didn't have to reveal her own. Carlos was no exception. He told her about growing up as the only brother of five sisters and the only son of parents who spoke little English. About how he'd always wanted kids, but his ex-wife was adamantly opposed. About how he dreamed of opening his own restaurant, believed in extraterrestrial life, and had once saved a man who was choking on a piece of steak. But about her own past, Brenda said little.

"All systems down," she told Kathryn the day after Carlos left her. They were at Kathryn's office after hours. Nearing fifty, Kathryn juggled her faculty position with a part-time private practice in Cole Valley, a long marriage, and two teenagers.

"When's the last time you talked to your mother?" Kathryn asked. She was drinking Scotch. Brenda wanted one.

"Let's not do this," Brenda said, standing at the window and watching a group of people board a city bus. Her mother called twice a year, from another public rehab program, from a craps table where she was up a few hundred and well into the free drinks, from a new boyfriend's truck, the wind whipping her phone so that her voice was barely audible as they raced across the Nevada desert.

"You send her a check each month," Kathryn said.

"This has nothing to do with her."

"You're pregnant, honey. Of course it does."

Next to her at the gate, Steve was talking to his daughter. "You know I'd do anything to be there," he said, rubbing his unshaven chin. Brenda could hear his daughter's crying through the phone. "Nothing's leaving DC, sweetie. Even if I could make it driving, they just shut 95 down."

"Brenda," a man said loudly from across the gate area.

She recognized his voice immediately, although she hadn't heard it in almost ten years. Briefly, she considered throwing her jacket over her head. Steve glanced at her expectantly.

Brenda forced a smile. "Hal," she said as the man—an ex boyfriend—approached. He was graying and had a beard, but looked fundamentally the same as he had in grad school.

"What are you doing here?" he asked smiling.

"I'm heading to Atlanta," she said, desperately trying to think of a way to escape.

"I've been in the Sudan. Working with the orphans," he volunteered, as if of course she would know what the meant. And she did. The story had been in the news for days: UN workers had found a group of fifty orphans living in a bombed out boot factory. Hal was a trauma specialist who got called in to situations like this. He'd been at 9/11, the Asian tsunami, the earthquake in Haiti, all the major catastrophes of the last decade.

She nodded. "Where's home these days?" she asked, as if she didn't periodically stalk him online and didn't already know that he lived in Boston, that he occasionally ran road races, that his children attended a pricey prep school.

He paused. "I'm separated, so home is whatever hotel room I'm in." He forced out a laugh. "Sarah and the kids are in Chicago with her parents for Christmas. I'm flying out to see them. We're trying to be civilized about it all." He was wearing cargo pants and a black parka, looking like an expedition leader on one of those ghastly wilderness survival programs.

He smiled again. "I'm going for coffee. Do you want to join me?"

"I'll watch your stuff," Steve offered. Brenda silently cursed him.

They ended up at a dimly-lit pub filled with men nursing

drinks. The only place open in their terminal, it smelled like a mildewed wet sponge and was decorated with dark furniture and British curios.

"This is grim," Brenda said.

Hal shrugged. "I'm still on Geneva time," he said, ordering a whiskey. Brenda got decaf.

"How are the orphans?" Brenda said. The children had been discovered only days before, when a wrecking crane arrived to demolish the factory. They had been there for six months and the older children ran a school for the younger ones. They'd figured out how to operate some of the factory's machines, and every child had a pair of boots made from scrap leather—neon green, hot pink, leopard print.

"How you'd expect. Some are doing remarkably, others will never recover."

"You're done exactly what you wanted to," she said.

"My Zen master warns against that kind of thinking.

Dear God, Brenda thought. "So you're Buddhist now?"

"You see enough suffering and you turn to either religion or alcohol."

"Or both," she said, nodding at his drink.

He laughed and took a sip.

"I've always had regrets about what happened with us, Brenda."

She paused. "We would have killed each other if we'd stayed together." He'd asked her out the first week of school. Back then, she'd thought the world would split apart at the seams when she first told him about her past—her father's death, her mother's drinking, their itinerant life, the holidays she'd spent alone since the age of eighteen. But he'd simply taken her hand and they had continued walking to his apartment. A week later he'd told her he loved her. During the entire year she'd dated Hal, their first of grad school—he had neglected to mention that he had a girlfriend in the PeaceCorps in Mongolia. When she'd surfaced, he'd left Brenda with no warning. Six months later, they'd been married.

At the bar, he put his hands up and his eyes twinkled. "I was a self-involved ass and I'm sorry. But I like to think I've evolved in the last decade. This"—he gestured between the two of them—"can't just be a coincidence." He paused and then looked her directly in the eye. "Nothing's going out today. I'm getting a hotel room." He paused. "I'd love it if you'd join me. Spend Christmas with me and then we'll go our separate ways"

She stared at him. The last time she'd seen him had been at their graduation, his wife pregnant by then. Besides Carlos, he was the only man she'd ever truly been in love with. She'd once felt that he had imprinted himself upon her, that he alone was equipped to reach into her chest and suture the wounds there. But years had passed and now she loved someone else and this man in front of her seemed like a complete tool.

She stood up. "I'm going back to my seat," she said, as if she was heading to an apartment across the city instead of a patch of industrial carpet ten yards away.

He didn't persist and when she returned to her seat Steve was on the phone with his daughter again. At noon, they cancelled Brenda's flight. Eighteen inches of snow had fallen, the worst blizzard on record in over a century. Interstate 95 was still shut down in both directions and the mayor of DC had declared a state of emergency.

She got in line at Customer Service and an hour later, approached the counter. "We can get you on a Saturday flight," the agent said, puff-eyed, tie loosened, one bad customer interaction away from losing it.

"That's five days from now," Brenda said.

"The first available flight is Saturday," he repeated in a neutral tone.

"Are you going to put me up in DC?"

"We can offer you $5 daily coupons for the food court."

"Can you get me back to San Francisco?"

He typed for a few seconds. "There's a flight a week from today with one open seat."

"I need to get out today."

He blinked. "Nothing's leaving today, ma'am. You're welcome to consider your options and then get in line again."

She glanced behind her at a line which snaked all the way to security. The woman next to her began to cry.

"Put me on the next flight to San Francisco."

He tapped away and then handed her a printout of her new itinerary. She looked up and saw Steve waving at her. "I'm getting a cab to a hotel. Wanna a ride?" She looked him up and down. He was probably 6'4" but he was a cop and he seemed harmless. She followed him.

"Closest hotel is twenty minutes out," the cab driver said in clipped, accented English as they stepped into the back seat. He had dark skin and a narrow build. An Ethiopian flag hung from his rear view mirror. Heat blasted as they inched through traffic to exit the airport. The cab's wipers flapped furiously at the snow.

"How's your daughter?" she asked Steve.

"She's a wreck. Of course my ex is stirring the pot. She wants her new husband to walk my daughter down the aisle." He rolled his eyes.

The cab started to skid and Steve's arm shot in front of Brenda and brushed her breasts. Even with his arm in front of her, she still bumped into the back of the passenger seat. The cabbie pulled them back into the center of the lane. "Everything's under control," he said in a tight voice, both hands tight on the wheel.

"Sorry about that," Steve said, blushing. "Are you ok?"

Brenda nodded and rubbed her shoulder. "I should have had this on," she said as she snapped her seatbelt. The canvas was uncomfortably tight against her waist. She looked out the window.

"I'm pregnant," she said and then couldn't believe she had.

"How far along?" Steve asked.

"Almost three months."

"That's great."

"It's not that simple," Brenda said.

"That guy at the airport?"

"He's an ex. I haven't seen him forever. The father left me"

"Bastard."

"He doesn't even know," she snorted and shook her head and tried not to cry.

"Me and my ex got married because she was pregnant. We'd been together three or four months, tops. Next thing you know, your kids are in high school, your wife's fallen out of love with you, your son's got a bad pot habit and your daughter's engaged to a kid who barely knows his elbow from his ass, but is about to ship out and you think, how exactly did we get here? I bust my ass every day but it's still like I'm asleep on the job. Believe me, I get it."

Brenda laughed and wiped her eyes. She looked more closely at Steve. Over the years, she'd seen a few cops as patients. They usually came to her because they had to, a referral after a trauma at work. She liked the hard patients: guys who'd been dragged or forced into counseling, people in recovery, teenagers who'd barely survived suicide attempts. She'd once wanted to do work like Hal's, base jumping into hot spots across the globe. But when she'd started her internships, it was longer-term counseling that she'd loved. "There's plenty of trauma in America," Kathryn had said when Brenda was choosing between a job offer in San Francisco and the fellowship in trauma psychology that Hal had already accepted.

The cab skidded to a stop in front of a Day's Inn with a view of an industrial park and the Beltway. Brenda and Steve booked the last two vacant rooms. In her room, Brenda cranked up the heat and pulled open the blinds. Snow was still falling. She put the TV on mute, lay on the bed and stared at her phone. Carlos would be well into Christmas with his family and Cassie by now, feeling, she could imagine, as if his life was beginning again, as if all those wretched nights in the months after his wife had cheated were now solely the province of the past. Chastened by disaster, but once again ready to go, like the crew of astronauts buckling in for the first post-Challenger launch. People start over all the time, she told herself.

She'd first been to DC when she was twelve, having won from the Kiwanas an all expense paid trip and scholarship for giving a speech about Benjamin Franklin. She and four other kids from Kentucky had converged on the city with scholarship recipients from across the country. They'd taken tours of Congress, the Supreme Court and, late one night, the maze of tunnels beneath the Lincoln Memorial. On the bus ride home, she'd daydreamed about moving to DC as an adult and imagined being married to a State Department official who looked very much like the English teacher who had encouraged her to apply for the Kiwanis scholarship and who would, later that night, drive her home and wait to pull away until she unlocked the door and stepped inside.

They were living in Covington, Kentucky, back then, renting a one-bedroom apartment in a building sandwiched between a McDonalds and a laundromat . She hardly thought of that time anymore. But she remembered that trip to DC and, today, in a motel room far from home, she remembered a winter blizzard, a day nearly as white as this one, on which she walked home from fourth grade in soaked canvas sneakers and an equally wet thrift-shop-winter coat, another kid's name scrawled in black magic marker on the label. A day on which she pushed open the door to their apartment expecting to find it cold, dark and empty, expecting to have hours to kill before her mother got home from the hotel where she cleaned rooms, but instead finding it brightly lit, with the heat blasting and mix brownies baking in the oven, hot chocolate on the stove, a Marvin Gaye song playing on the alarm clock they used as a radio. With her mother smiling and there, as she rarely was, waiting for her.

That night the Covington boyfriend didn't hammer on the door demanding to be let in, his fist cocked when he finally was; the landlord didn't call with another threat to evict them; and her mother didn't drink, or even cry. That night, she fell asleep in her mother's arms on the couch, lulled by the sounds of late night television, and she woke up the next morning feeling as if the world had steadied itself, as if she could catch her breath. Her father had been dead seven years by then and although Brenda thought about him, she'd learned not to bring him up. It had been a car accident. Maybe he'd been drinking, maybe not. After the funeral, her mother never mentioned her father again and, on the whole, lived as if the past had never happened at all. Brenda could run through her mother's boyfriends like they were the starting lineup of a baseball team, but she could barely summon up an image of her father beyond the smell of cigarettes and Juicy Fruit gum, the stubble on this cheeks, and the sawdust on his pants from running the chop saw at a timber yard.

For years, as they moved to Knoxville, St. Louis, Denver, and finally Reno, she had held onto the feeling of that snow day as tightly as you might a friend's hand in a dark theater, your eyes squeezed almost shut, the gleaming blade of the serial killer's knife suspended above his next victim's still-thumping heart. *Sure*, she had allowed once with Kathryn, *you could call it terror.* Who could blame her for playing it safe, building a life in which she expected neither pounding at the door nor the sound of a key being turned by someone you trusted enough to give one to, a life in which solitude's steady yields far outstripped love's untenable risks.

Laying there, she thought about Hal too. They used to talk about the practice they'd open together doing just the kind of work he now was. She thought of the orphans he'd been with and could see small dirty toenails, dark gaps where baby teeth had been, the jagged nubs of adult incisors rupturing the surface of their gums, pee-stained underwear, the elastic bands shot. All of those problems could be taken care of with a hot bath, a change of clothes, a good meal. It was what you couldn't see that so threatened the kids.

These were the lives she hadn't chosen, the one in which, like Hal—or with Hal—she'd tracked a swath of trauma across the globe. Rwanda. Sudan. The Congo. Or the life in which she'd been more her mother's daughter, in which she'd craved the feeling of being drunk rather than been terrified by it, in which she chose involvements with the wrong men over solitude. Or now, the one in which Carlos' wife had never begged him to come back, in which she'd had the courage to tell him the truth, in which he'd reacted with the joy he possessed in such abundance and had held her hand during her most recent ultrasound. These were nothing more than phantom lives, but right then, they felt almost real, and certainly as real as what was happening second by second in her body, the rapidly-dividing cells that would become either a full-fledged life or a ruined mass in a red biohazard bag.

The week after Carlos had broken up with her, she hadn't been able to sleep. Instead, she paced her apartment trying to decide what to do. Tell him or not. Abort or keep the baby. In that harried, half-conscious state, she'd kept stumbling across evidence of him. Too many of his things—inconsequential, but still his— were at her apartment, like patches of ice that would not melt. His spare inhaler on the bedside table, his razor in the bathroom, a graphic novel he'd lent her after their first date on the coffee table. She had boxed it all up and, without a note, sent it to the restaurant where he worked.

At six, Steve knocked on her door, showered, shaved, doused in cologne, dressed in a black tuxedo and holding his laptop. She raised her eyebrows.

"My son figured it out. He's going to film it on his webcam and then set up his laptop at the reception so I can talk to people." He shrugged. "Clever kid when he's not stoned."

Brenda laughed. "Give me a minute," she said, re-emerging with fresh perfume and lipstick applied.

At the bar, Steve ordered a bottle of champagne and enlarged the screen on his computer. His daughter appeared in her wedding dress, maybe 5'2" with his Italian looks. As she approached her brother, she gestured angrily for him to put the computer away. Then she saw the screen.

"Daddy," she yelled.

He wiped his eyes and waved at her. "I love you, baby girl."

His daughter took her brother's arm and they walked down the aisle on the beach, a red cloth spread on white sand. Rows of people stood up from folding white chairs, most of them barefoot. Steve stood up at the bar and shook his head, wiping his eyes again.

The bartender was wearing a santa hat and a cheap tux. The

bar was crowded with travelers whose plans had been derailed. A row of people at the bar—a plump middle aged woman with a reindeer sweater, a handsome black man in his twenties, an older couple with matching haircuts—gladly accepted glasses of champagne when Steve bought two more bottles.

Brenda saw Hal sitting at a corner table plucking away on his laptop, his phone on the table, a whiskey in front of him. He had shaved and had changed into a grey sweater and jeans. But he looked lost and uncertain. This would be his kids' first Christmas without him. Seeing him was like walking through an apartment she'd lived in as a child, an innocence she'd once possessed ghosting her from room to room. She knew Hal's secrets—his guilt over his brother's drowning death during childhood, his self-consciousness about the size of his penis. Now she knew Carlos' too, and both men knew hers.

At the bar, Steve raised his glass and his voice to be heard over the music. "To my daughter and her new husband," he said proudly. He turned toward Brenda. "And to Brenda, who's having a baby." He threw a thick arm around her and kissed her on the cheek, his lips warm and not unwelcome. People at the bar smiled at her and raised their plastic flutes. From across the bar, Hal did the same, cocking his head and holding her gaze.

She excused herself, walking through the empty lobby and then outside. The air was still freezing but the snow had finally stopped. She dialed her mother's number and listened as it rang a dozen times. She finally hung up and then called her grandmother, who picked up right away. "Boy, I missed you today, sweetie," her grandmother said. "You would have loved it. The kids chipped in and got me a flat screen and I'm sitting here eating popcorn and drinking Chardonnay and feeling like a queen."

"I'm pregnant," Brenda said.

There was a pause. 'Oh Lord, I'm going to be a great grand-ma. I know you think I'm just this crazy old lady. But there hasn't been a day in the last thirty years that I didn't miss you. It broke my heart when your momma took you away."

Brenda took a breath. She wasn't used to this kind of talk. A snow plow rolled past the hotel. Her skin ached from the cold.

"Is it a boy or a girl?" her grandmother asked.

"I don't know," Brenda said.

"When can I come visit? We'll need to set you up a nursery."

They talked for a few more minutes and then hung up.

This is how you do it then, Brenda thought as she walked back inside. Her mother chose to run. Hal chose Sarah. She chose Carlos but he chose his ex. Now, she chose this.

That she could finally see a way forward—a flash of images, like a newsreel, a dream—was answer enough. Kathryn would coach her through labor and stay with her for a few weeks. Her own mother would resurface and hold this baby as she once had Brenda, taking her best shot at love and again missing, her heart corroded like an old faucet, capable of producing nothing more than a messy, ferrous trickle. Her grandmother would visit and then she and the baby would go to Georgia, maybe next Christmas. Each of them would be who they'd always been: nothing more, nothing less.

She walked past the bar and went up to her room, which felt vacant and clean, utterly free of memories or habits. She knew Hal would knock on her door later that night but didn't yet know if she would let him in.

The TV was on mute but the room was otherwise dark. She turned up the heat, stripped off her clothes and stretched out naked on the king size mattress. Her phone rang. It was Carlos. She could see him slipping out the kitchen door at his parents', wagering no one would miss him for a few minutes, lighting a cigarette as he dialed her number.

But she didn't answer and finally the ringing stopped. She knew then that she wouldn't tell him. She would let him continue down the path he'd chosen. This secret, she would keep. It would become an unspoken part of her past, an unknown part of his.

HIT ME

Weasel keeps certain secrets from Ruthie. He must. He is, after all, interested and she is his Case Manager. But still, he betrays himself. It's an old habit, one he can't help. They meet every Thursday in a corner office on the eighth floor of the Liberty Building in downtown Oakland. Having observed that Ruthie is a woman who craves order but pretends to embrace chaos, Weasel is always on time for these appointments. To please her, he will do this. But he will not talk about his childhood, the fact that he is still using, or his HIV status. They do, however, discuss the merits of sobriety, his job search, and, because Ruthie was trained in a school of therapy that advises selective disclosure, her pending divorce.

If pushed, Weasel will say that his mother is a proud woman and, although it is not true, he will tell Ruthie that she was diagnosed with breast cancer a few years ago. His father is a blank stare. When asked about his brother, a plumber named Lonny, Weasel laughs. Ruthie keeps a framed picture of her son on her desk; until three months ago, there was also a picture of her husband, a sunburned man with thinning blond hair. Based on the photo and the divorce, Weasel is pretty sure he's a fag.

Often during their sessions, things break. Walking into her office, Ruthie's shoulder will brush a framed diploma on the wall and it will crash to the floor, shattering. Reaching for a paper clip, she'll knock a lamp off her desk. Accidents find her, she explains, the way mosquitoes seek out whomever in a group produces the most carbon dioxide. As evidence, she can point to the missing joint on her left index finger and a six-inch scar on her right shin.

You gotta be careful, Ruthie, Weasel will say as he leans down and brushes the shards of a broken light bulb onto a piece of paper. *You're starting to look like a fighter. Like Ali's daughter— what's her name. I used to box, you know.*

With that, he'll stand up and start shadowboxing, circling her desk, batting at the literacy poster on her wall of Shaquille O'Neal poring over a book in his Lakers uniform. *Take that, big boy,* he'll say, batting at Shaquille's massive, smiling face. Ruthie will push her chair back from her desk and laugh and Weasel will, for an instant, feel good.

Leaving her office, Weasel walks through a room full of men waiting for appointments with women like Ruthie. The building is smoke-free but no one cares and the smell mixes thickly with the sharp musk of unwashed bodies. The room is never quiet, filled instead with the sounds of a hacking cough, a man muttering to himself, a magazine's pages being turned.

Weasel heads to the 19th Street BART Station and waits for his brother to pick him up. They will stop at Boston Market for the Family Deal and then, as they have been doing every week since Weasel got out of the inpatient rehab unit at UCSF nine months earlier, head to the apartment complex in San Rafael where their mother lives. Weasel leans against a parking meter. A woman carrying a fat baby and a sleek diaper bag emerges from the BART station. When he smiles at her, she scowls and hurries past.

Lonny pulls up at six, his pick up idling by the curb. Weasel puts out his cigarette and swings into the passenger seat.

"Hi, Robbie." Lonny refuses to call his baby brother Weasel, the name he chose for himself at a NA retreat. At forty-one,

Lonny is a divorced father and is newly in love with a woman named Susan whom he met at Safeway. She was buying a pint of sugar-free coconut ice cream and he was buying a bottle of Grecian Formula. He had never seen her before and so what he saw was a woman who seemed to be alone and who looked open to the possibility of him. *I like coconut ice cream*, he had said to her as he covered the label of his hair tonic with a large, capable hand and cursed a lifelong inability to improvise.

Lonny had wanted Susan to come along for dinner tonight, but she wasn't ready. He had tried to explain that his brother would spend most of the night flirting with her and his mother would like her as long as she said something nice about the newly renovated bathroom.

"You still fucking that Chinese girl?" Weasel wedges his boots against the dash and slumps into the passenger seat.

"Her name is Susan." Lonny says. "And she's Korean."

Weasel lights another cigarette and then offers one to his brother. Lonny shakes his head and rolls his window down as he pulls back into traffic. Weasel exhales. "She ever been with a black man before?"

"Fuck you."

Although they look alike—the same broad shoulders, full lips, and green eyes—they are actually half brothers. Same mother, different fathers. Their mother, Louise Candor, is Irish on both sides, with the eyes that her boys inherited and thinning hair she dyes a red it never actually was. Her first husband, Slim, was Lonny's father, a black postal worker who had grown up down the block from her in Newark. Weasel's father, Lou, came into the picture a year after Slim left Louise. Lou was a Brooklyn Italian who ran a bar in West Trenton until a distant cousin offered him a job managing a seafood restaurant in San Francisco. Weasel was three weeks old when they left the East

Coast, crammed into the cab of a rental truck that never went over 55. Two weeks later, the family moved into a one-bedroom in the Haight.

Tonight, Lonny and Weasel walk down the dimly-lit carpeted hall towards their mother's apartment. Early June and her door is still decorated for Easter, with sun-bleached cardboard eggs, a fringe of hula grass, and a wicker basket velcroed to it. Lonny knocks, but there's no response. He knocks again and presses his ear against the door, his heart starting to race. Each week, he worries that they're going to show up and find her dead. At the sound of approaching steps, Weasel peers down the darkened hall.

But it's not their mother. It's her neighbor, Ella. All ninety-five pounds of her, wearing a bathing suit, a white robe, and aqua socks.

"Boys," she says, a hint of flirtation in her voice.

"Good evening, Ms. Ella." Lonny, as usual, does the talking for them.

"Your mama's gone."

"She's supposed to have dinner with us."

"She went to Reno to play blackjack. She skipped water aerobics to catch the five o'clock bus. It's senior night at Bally's." Ella shrugs and busies herself unlocking her deadbolt.

Lonny stares at the bags of food Weasel is carrying. "You want to join us, Ms. Ella?"

"Can't. I've got a date with Mr. Rollins in 5-C."

Weasel swallows a grin as Lonny opens the apartment with his spare key. Inside, Weasel empties the bags of food onto the kitchen table, his hands sticky with spilled gravy and melted butter. Even though Weasel hasn't eaten for twenty-four hours and Lonny has spent all afternoon sweating under an industrial sink in the kitchen of an Italian restaurant, there's still too much food for the two of them. The knowledge that they will be left staring at half-emptied Styrofoam containers makes Weasel lonely, makes him briefly wonder why these dinners don't include more people—Lonny's daughter, or that cousin over in Daly City whom they never see.

Weasel cracks open a can of Coke. "So what's the story with Susan?"

"She's a nurse at Oakland Children's. She works with cancer kids."

"That's cheerful."

"She's good with kids."

"Has Lisa met her?" Weasel asks.

"Lisa's going through a phase."

"Daddy's little girl." Weasel smiles. He adores his neice.

"Something like that."

"I met a girl," Weasel says. "Her name's Ruthie."

Lonny looks up from his plate.

"She's a stripper. She used to live at the Playboy Mansion."

Lonny laughs.

"She's splitting up with her old man. I'm taking her out Saturday."

Lonny raises an eyebrow.

Weasel has to watch himself around his brother. It's been easy enough to keep his using from his sponsor, his NA buddies, his doctor and certainly from Ruthie. But it's different with Lonny. He's not stupid, or naive, even with all his efforts to camouflage himself against a background of domestic routines—coaching Lisa's basketball team, wearing, even on weekends, golf shirts which feature his plumbing company's logo, changing the oil in his truck every 3,000 miles.

Tuesday and Thursday nights, Weasel locks the door of the room he rents week to week, turns on the radio, and lowers the shades. He buys the stuff on Sundays and lets it sit, gathering a thin layer of dust. He keeps to this schedule to prove to himself that his relationship with heroin has evolved. It has gone from a deep, constant hunger to a twice-weekly choice. And tonight, when he gets home from dinner, it will be there for him.

Waiting is new to him. It makes him feel like one of those revirginated evangelical types he's heard about, someone who's in love enough to wait for sex. He knows his sponsor would tear this logic apart. *The beloved is to smack as sex is to high . . . is that what you're saying? Just twice a week? Junkies either die or get clean. You know that.*

"I didn't know Mom played blackjack. I thought she stuck to the nickel slots." Weasel says as he reaches for another piece of cornbread.

"She and Dad used to play," Lonny says, referring to his stepfather, Weasel's dad.

Weasel looks up. "Does she ever win?" The apartment is stuffy and even with the overhead fan on, beads of sweat stream down Weasel's smooth, pink scalp.

Lonny shrugs. "She knows when to stop. If she's having a bad night, she comes home."

"How much has she won?"

"Who knows," Lonny says.

"C'mon. How much?"

"It's all tied up in CDs and bonds. Five years ago, I told her, Ma, play with it a little, look into some of the high-tech stocks. I researched a few companies for her, but she wouldn't budge. She just kept saying, *it'll crash, it'll crash.* She would've made a killing if she'd let me invest it for her."

"How much are we talking about?" Weasel asks.

"I don't even know. Somewhere over $100,000, I think." Lonny knows this is a mistake. But he can't shake the gut feeling that it really is different this time. That, as Weasel has asserted with that blend of self-loathing and candor that makes Lonny cringe, the sixth visit to rehab is the charm.

"And she's living like this?" Weasel surveys the small living room and laughs, trying to keep the bitterness out of his voice. All that money sitting there, and he barely has enough to eat.

"She's happy here. Look, don't say a word about this."

"Right," Weasel shovels in a bite of mashed potatoes. He can't stand the way his brother is watching him, the obvious effort Lonny is making to pretend this is a casual conversation.

The first time Weasel stole from his mother, it wasn't for drugs. He was boxing and he needed the cash to enter a tournament in Vegas. His mother had forbidden him from competing. She hated the sport and had already forced Lonny to give it up. But Weasel was a better fighter than Lonny. He had the perfect body for a middleweight and, unlike his brother, an appetite for training. They trained at a gym in the Mission with a coach named Mr. Freddy, a wiry loner who boxed for the Army during the Korean War. Where Lonny would put in a cursory two hours at the gym, Weasel would last for four and then run the long way home, through Golden Gate Park and the Sunset.

Weasel had one shot at going pro. He'd won six straight tournaments and Mr. Freddy had had a few promising conversations with a promoter from LA. The Vegas tournament was his audition. He needed the entry fee, bus fare, a hotel room, and, Mr. Freddy explained, a little extra to grease the wheels. Lonny was broke, but Mr. Freddy spotted him fifty bucks and Weasel put in what he'd saved from his job stocking shelves at a grocery store. He was still $200 short. So, he took a hundred dollars and his mother's wedding ring when she was at work one day. It had been years since any of them had heard from his father and he figured there was no way she'd miss it.

In the title fight, he was matched up against a kid from Boston named Donnelly. At five-nine, Donnelly was an even 160 and was chiseled like an action figure. He had a trainer, a coach, a girlfriend, and a robe that matched his golden trunks. Weasel had Mr. Freddy, Lonny, and shorts that were two sizes too big.

But Donnelly was also missing part of his chest. Mr. Freddy had heard that there'd been some kind of freak accident when he was a baby and that the doctors had taken out one of his pectoral muscles. On the right side of his chest, where the smooth, convex plate of the muscle should have been, his skin was sunken and coated with the iridescent glaze of scar tissue. It looked like a meteor the size of a human head had crashed there.

Weasel liked it when his opponents got cut. The blood made him want to hit harder. But there was something different about fighting someone with scars like that. Donnelly's wrecked chest was transfixing; it made him seem almost invincible. He wore the frailty that all fighters try so hard to disguise like a banner: perfection bleeding into ruin, the two states feeding off each other. It was as if, early on—too early—his body had taken a cruel, inoculating blow and now, long on the other side of that impact, Donnelly had nothing to be afraid of anymore.

Weasel talked himself out of a win and into a clean, fifth round knockout. Through his swollen eyes, he watched Donnelly accept the congratulations of the promoter who had been scouting them both. Weasel fought in a few more tournaments. But Las Vegas was it. He knew it and Mr. Freddy knew it and eventually, even the relentlessly optimistic Lonny got it.

"I'm thinking about getting back into boxing," Weasel says, putting down his plastic fork.

"Fighting?" Lonny looks up from his plate.

"No. Coaching girls."

"You're gonna coach girls' boxing?"

"It's gonna be big."

"Big money?"

"Eventually, yeah. Right now it's the idea. It's radical."

"What the hell are you talking about?"

"Think about it. It cuts through all the shit about women this, men that. There's a market out there. Chicks in the ring." He takes a quick jab at an imaginary opponent.

"Where are you going to teach these classes?" Lonny gets another Coke from the fridge. He won't drink around Weasel.

"I'm gonna get licensed as a personal trainer and then get a job at a gym. Then I'm gonna open my own place." He's up on his feet now and in one step he moves from the worn linoleum of their mother's kitchen to the carpet of the living room. He's working his arms, crouching low, his head bobbing like a loose joint. "C'mon. Let's go a few rounds." Weasel bends down and lifts the coffee table. The *TV Guide* and remote slip to the carpet, along with an empty ashtray.

"Settle down, Robbie."

"Let's go, Lonny." Weasel is dripping now and he pulls off his T-shirt. His skin is loose from the pounds he's dropped recently, but the muscles are still there. And with them, a long, new scar, running from his right nipple to the bottom of his rib cage.

Lonny takes a bite of chicken and tries to ignore the scar and the nagging feeling he has that Weasel is off his HIV cocktail.

"Get off your ass, old man," Weasel says as he drags the armchair to the corner of the room, blocking the TV with it. Deep depressions from the furniture pock the stiff gray carpet, a rectangle with the dimensions of a king sized bed. Lonny surveys the makeshift ring and, against his better judgment, stands up. "One round," he says.

"Old rules." Weasel says.

"Nothing in the face."

"Relax, pretty boy."

Lonny takes off his watch and rolls up the sleeves of his work shirt. "Ready?"

They circle each other slowly, easing back into the memory of the hours they spent sparring under Mr. Freddy's watchful eye. Weasel throws the first punch, a simple hook intended to test his brother's reflexes. Lonny grins, ducks, and delivers a quick, solid punch to Weasel's gut. Weasel retreats a step, fakes right, and then lands an uppercut on Lonny's neck.

"No face," Lonny protests.

"That was your neck."

Lonny swipes at Weasel's right ear, which juts out from his head, as pink and protrusive as a chimp's. Already, they are both out of breath and a sweat stain is spilling across Lonny's shirt.

There were years when Weasel was living in Golden Gate Park and, once a week, he would call Lonny demanding cash. Against the backdrop of Lisa's colicky cries, Lonny would refuse and as he heard the word "no" come out of his mouth, he would steel himself to the remorse that was already spreading through his body. After these conversations, he was inconsolable. Slow and stupid at work, impatient with Lisa and his wife.

Every few weeks, he would go looking for Weasel, dressed like a thug, a BART card and no wallet in his pocket, a backpack full of socks, underwear, sandwiches, soap, a razor. He would wander the streets of the Tenderloin, asking after Robbie, Robbie Candor. Who, if found, was either high and untouchable or worse.

I don't want fucking dental floss. I need cash. What do you think, you're some sainted outreach worker? Weasel would taunt as he patted Lonny down, searching for the bulge of his wallet.

Lonny would stand there, paralyzed by the desperate flicker of his brother's eyes and holding his breath to avoid the smell of Weasel's body—the sweat and shit and infection and his awful rotting breath. He would wait for Weasel to wear himself out with the shouting and the groping, to accept the fact that there was no money, that Lonny had come with nothing except his own futile desire to somehow make things better.

Now, they circle each other on the carpet. Weasel's knuckles are raw. They are grinning and then serious, lost in the old, familiar motions of their bodies. It's Lonny who breaks the rules first, landing a punch to his brother's already crooked nose.

"Bitch," Weasel grins and shakes the punch off.

"Oops." Lonny shrugs and the casualness of this gesture seems to Weasel an indication that his honor bound brother may have finally grasped the idea that certain rules can be broken.

Lonny jabs at Weasel's cheek and Weasel ducks, leans back, and then steadies himself. He's got Lonny tired now, his feet shuffling, his breathing labored. Weasel pummels his brother's torso, his shoulders churning, his head tucked low. Lonny's body is soft and hitting him feels like pounding a mattress. As his punches acquire a rhythm he hasn't felt for years, it's like he's back in the ring again, fighting the Boston kid, already certain that he is going to lose. He launches a punch into the strange cavity of his opponent's chest. But his fist keeps going and he thinks it's going to shoot straight through the kid's body. When he finally makes contact, he stumbles and the kid, who is used to fighters seeking out precisely what seems weakest about him, lands the deadening uppercut that has become his signature.

Lonny backs up to the corner of the carpet and tries to shove Weasel away from him. Their bodies tangle and they lean heavily into each other. Lonny wrestles free and sidesteps Weasel, getting some distance from him.

They stare at each other and, for a second, they both fear that they have gone too far. Lonny's gut aches, not from his brother's fists, but from a cocktail of sadness and regret. There are moments when he looks at his brother's face and still sees in it the kid he was, the one who couldn't sit still, who silently absorbed his father's rage, who couldn't bear to lose any game at all, who even competed to see who could pee faster.

Weasel knows how tenuous everything still is. But he also imagines that, maybe this one time, Lonny will understand. Understand that five days out of seven, Weasel plays by the rules. Understand that he has found a system that works for him. He uses a clean kit, he buys pure shit, no one else is involved. What else can he do? He has always wanted—still wants—more than the world is prepared to give him. And so he went, years ago, and found himself another world. He is being as safe as a man like him can stand to be.

He raises his arms in the air and prances to the other side of the carpet, shaking his retreating butt at Lonny. "Weasel Candor is back," he intones in his best Cosell imitation. "Bald, fat, and merciless."

Lonny chuckles as he unbuttons his sweat-stained shirt. It is not a full-blown laugh. But it is enough for Weasel, whose pounding heart begins to relax.

**

An hour later, Lonny drops Weasel off in downtown Oakland, hands him a crisp twenty, and then drives home to the one-bedroom bungalow he rents. There, he strips and showers, gingerly soaping his already aching muscles. As he dries off, he calls Susan, who answers on the first ring.

Lonny stares into the bathroom mirror as she talks about her day. And when she asks how dinner went, he tells her how there, amidst the half-empty containers of mashed potatoes and collard greens and the scattered chicken bones which they'd sucked clean, he and his brother lay on the floor, their heads touching, their feet pointed in opposite directions, their bare chests heaving. Weasel's nose was running and Lonny's eye was already starting to swell shut. When they finally struggled back up to their feet, they laughed at the stains left on the carpet, shapes that suggested their bodies like the bold, childish chalk lines of a crime scene.

Lonny keeps talking, lured into revelation by the quiet hum of the phone, by Susan's steady breathing on the other end. He tells her that fighting like this with Weasel, like they used to before they knew what real damage was, makes it feel like his brother is going to be okay this time. Looking at his reflection, he fingers the swollen, dark tissue of his eyelid and he tells her that, tonight, it finally feels like they've made it to the other side.

Across town, naked, and leaning against his kitchen sink, Weasel is searching. Patient fingers running along his skin, a cartographer scanning a battered, familiar map. The needle, freshly ripped out of its package, rests between the index and middle fingers of his free hand like a cigarette. He had a friend who used to shoot up into his neck with his eyes closed. Had a girlfriend who had used her cooch. Veins, no matter where they are, are just a way in.

His mind wanders. He imagines that, three hours north, at a blackjack table near the bar, his mother is having a good night. "Hit me," she'd say evenly, nodding at the dealer and glancing at her hand. She's already up five hundred. The dealer slaps a four on the table, and she nods. Next to her, a man in a cheap suit sips from his club soda, grunts softly and folds when he's dealt a queen. Weasel can see his mother walking away from the table, already eyeing her next target, a purse full of chips rattling against her bad hip. No one always knows when to stop.

Weasel laughs. At the idea of his mother hoarding all that money. At the quiet triumph of finding a decent vein wedged between his big and second toes.

**

From across the Blockbuster, Ruthie sees Weasel walk into the store. He is with a black girl who can't be more than twelve. Ruthie curses under her breath and, as Weasel and the girl walk towards the New Releases section, she ducks behind a larger than life cardboard cutout of Jackie Chan. It is Friday night now, just before eleven, and the store will close in ten minutes. But she's still empty-handed.

"No way, Lisa." She hears his voice first. She peers through the crack of Jackie Chan's armpit. Weasel stands next to the girl, his arms crossed across his chest. He is wearing a white under-shirt and jeans. He needs a shave.

Lisa grabs another video.

"No stalker movies." He takes the case from her and places it back on the shelf.

"I already saw it anyway. *With Dad*."

He gently grabs her shoulders and pivots her away from the shelf, pushing her along.

Ruthie looks at her watch. There's still time to find a decent movie and escape without Weasel's spotting her. It has been a terrible day and a worse night. Her boss made another pass at her and a client fired her, to the extent that someone getting free therapy can do so. Then, her almost-ex husband came to pick up their son for the weekend with divorce papers in hand. In the hours since then, she has worked her way through most of a six-pack and a frozen pizza. And so, rather than doing what she should do—which is to let Weasel choose whether or not to approach her—she is instead spying on her client, unable to take her eyes off his broad shoulders and the tapered v of his back.

"We *gotta* get Booty Call II." Lisa's voice rings loudly through the store.

"No," Weasel says.

But Lisa has already rounded the corner, heading straight towards the Bs. Following her, Weasel looks up at the sound of someone cursing and sees Ruthie crashing to the floor on top of the cardboard Jackie Chan.

His heart races. He can't help it.

He watches as Ruthie pushes herself up from the industrial grade carpet, her feet getting tangled once again with the poster. Her hair is pulled back and she is wearing tight, faded jeans and a navy hooded Berkeley sweatshirt. This is who she is at home, he thinks. *This* is the Ruthie he wants to know, the Friday night, pint of ice cream, stack of videos, sunk deep into the couch Ruthie. The just woken up, Saturday morning, hot coffee, barefoot Ruthie.

"Are you OK?" he asks.

She looks up and he watches her eyes closely. Her face is blank, neutral, nothing. His heart sinks.

Back on her feet, she straightens her hair. "How are you, Robbie?"

"I'm here with my niece." He gestures towards Lisa, who is now holding a stack of three videos.

Ruthie turns toward the girl and looks at her more closely. She has the same green eyes as Weasel. Her braids are tight, like they were just done, and she holds herself like an athlete. A little chunky, the way girls her age often are.

"Uh, Lisa, this is Ruthie. She's a friend of mine." As soon as he says it, he curses himself. *Friend?* He shoves his hands into his front pockets and clenches his fists.

"Find anything good there?" Ruthie nods toward the videos.

"Probably not. C'mon, Lisa, your dad's waiting." Weasel steps around Ruthie, brushing her arm lightly, and puts his hand on Lisa's shoulder. He backs away, toward the counter, pulling Lisa with him.

"Have a good weekend." Ruthie says, and then cringes at how canned she sounds.

In response, he offers a nod and then turns away. But Ruthie doesn't. Instead, she watches as his shoulders sag slightly and a hot flushed red travels up his neck.

**

Louise Candor does not show her sons up twice. She has dinner waiting for them when they arrive the next week. Pork chops, lima beans, microwaved dinner rolls, apple pie, iced tea.

Lonny, up last night until three with Susan, is too exhausted and hungry to play the role of translator between his brother and mother. He sits down to the table and devotes all of his attention to the food in front of him.

"I got a job interview on Monday. At 24-Hour Fitness, that one over on Montgomery," Weasel announces as he reaches across Lonny's plate for another roll.

"You takin' your pills, Robbie?"

"Yeah, Ma. Did you hear me that I got an interview?"

"What are you going to do at a gym?" Louise doesn't look up from her plate.

"Teach classes."

"Water aerobics?"

"No, Ma." He glances at Lonny who is trying to hide his smile. "Boxing. Women's boxing."

"What do you want to do that for?"

"It's my most marketable skill," Weasel says.

Lonny laughs through a mouthful of pork.

"Plus they pay good," Weasel adds.

"Benefits?" Louise looks up.

"No. But once I build up a clientele, I can open my own gym."

"You should look for a job with benefits. Like your brother. What if something happens to you?" This is as close as she will come to discussing his health.

"Nothing's happening to anyone, Ma." Lonny, onto his second plate, is eager to change the subject.

An hour later, as they walk across the parking lot towards Lonny's truck, Weasel offers to drive. Lonny shakes his head and climbs in behind the wheel. Weasel rolls his window down and then back up. He plays a drum roll on the glove compartment. Lonny reaches out and puts a hand on Weasel's forearm to still him.

"You remember that kid I fought in Vegas?" Weasel asks.

"Sure. Mark Donnelly."

"I think about him sometimes."

"You could've beaten him."

"That's not what I'm talking about. I've been meditating on him. You know, for NA. The thing I can't figure out is why he got into the ring in the first place. He was missing half his chest. Hell, I bet he fought with his shirt on for the first few years, before he figured out it would do him more good to let it all hang out. That's the freakiest scar I've ever seen, and trust me, I've seen my share." Weasel reaches into his front pocket for a crushed pack of Marlboros. He fishes one out and lights it. He rolls down the window and flicks the empty matchbook onto the street.

"If Mom loaned me $50,000, I could start my own gym," he says.

"Not an option," Lonny says.

They drive in silence for a few minutes and Weasel stares out at the dark water of the Bay and the parade of oncoming head-lights' flooding them as they pass over the Richmond Bridge. "Will you talk to her for me?" he asks. There was a time when Lonny would have done anything to keep Weasel clean; now, Weasel knows, he'll do almost anything.

"I can't," Lonny says.

Weasel leans his temple against the window and closes his eyes. He knows he has to play this just right. It's a tricky combi-nation. He stays quiet.

"I'm sorry, Robbie." Lonny reaches to turn the radio on and then thinks better of it.

But Weasel is already gone. In his mind, he is far away from Lonny, retreating to a place where he has no need for luck or a decent break or a mother or a brother willing to take a risk on him. This place—foot perched on the sink; subterranean tunnel of a vein; slip of the eyes; jungle flutter of wings—this place isn't, he knows, all the way real. But, once you've been there, how could anyone stay away?

They ride in silence for ten minutes and when they hit Jef-ferson, Weasel asks to be dropped off in front of a mini-mart. Lonny offers to wait and then drive him to his place, but Weasel shrugs as he gets out of the truck and steps onto the street.

Lonny pulls back into traffic and tries to forget about his brother. But before he is even halfway to Susan's, he is turning the truck around. He wants to make it up to his brother, thinks maybe he can talk Robbie into joining him and Susan at the jazz bar they're going to.

He's never been to Weasel's room before, but he remembers that it's in the Hotel Buena Vista. Ten minutes later, he's double parked in front of a narrow alley next to the hotel, a five-story building with crumbling stucco walls and black metal bars on the windows. He thinks how terrible it would be to come home to this place every night and then feels guilty. It's the nicest place his brother has lived in years.

Lonny approaches the front desk, tapping on the scratched Plexiglas window to get the clerk's attention. The man briefly consults a clipboard and then returns his gaze to a small television as he tells Lonny that Robert Candor is in room 306.

Lonny decides against the elevator, with its tagged, battered doors, and heads instead to the stairwell. On the third floor, he wanders down a dark hall, beneath sputtering, dim overhead lights. The maroon carpet smells from years' worth of spilled beer, smoke, and piss. Music and voices flow out from each door he passes—hip hop, salsa, English, Spanish, Russian.

As he turns the corner, Lonny's body stiffens. This is how it's always been when he gets too close to Weasel's life; it feels as if he is just a moment away from losing everything. Lonny has never tried anything more than pot, but deep down he knows that he is not so different from his brother. It's just that he has spent a lifetime burying the very impulses that Weasel has never been able to resist.

Lonny knocks on the door to room 306. The off-white paint is chipped and stained and a handmade sticker for a band he's never heard of is pasted below the peephole. He knocks again and when there is still no response, he tests the door, expecting to find it locked. But it opens easily and as he steps across the threshold, he calls out his brother's name.

It takes only a few seconds to survey the room. The space couldn't be larger than twelve-by-twelve, with an efficiency kitchen along one wall and peeling linoleum flooring. There are two windows, one of them cracked open. On the right wall, there is a door that must lead to the bathroom. Two black garbage bags overflowing with clothes are shoved into a corner. There's an unplugged iron set on a laminated chipboard card table and next to it, a thirteen-inch TV. A crusty red towel hangs over the back of a solitary plastic lawn chair, which is shoved against the table.

But these are just the details. What matters is the single, stripped mattress in the far corner of the room and the body collapsed on it. Weasel is wearing only his boxers and his body looks limp and wet, as if he has washed up on shore. His eyes are closed and the needle is on the floor next to him.

Lonny is dizzy with rage. "Get up," he barks as he strides across the room.

Weasel is unresponsive.

"Get the fuck up." Lonny is leaning over Weasel now. He kicks the side of the mattress. Weasel's body jerks in response to the impact and his eyes flick open and then shut again.

"How long?" Lonny is leaning over him now, hissing into his ear.

Weasel turns toward the wall, offering Lonny the pale slope of his bare back.

"That's it, Robbie. I can't do this again. You're on your own."

Weasel tries to grab his brother's leg, but he misses and instead his palm hits the floor. He is only vaguely aware of the pressure of Lonny's fingers on his neck, checking his pulse. Even less aware of the sound of his brother storming out of the room, slamming the door shut behind him, and then gone.

**

Ruthie knows there's no point trying to hide it. She has been crying too hard. Puffy eyes, blotchy cheeks, fibers of tissue stuck to her shirt. She stares at the mirror and starts to cry again as a woman, a new client of hers, steps out of the end stall. The woman does a double take and rushes out of the bathroom.

They do one night clinic a week, and it's always packed. Weasel's probably already sitting in the crowded waiting room. There is something relentless about his punctuality. Especially considering the fact that he bullshits his way through their sessions. She is certain he's relapsed, although she will not bring it up today. She'd put a call into his doctor at the UCSF HIV Clinic earlier in the day to check, but hadn't heard back yet. Her only goals for the remainder of the day are not to cry again and to somehow purge herself of her attraction for Weasel. The transparency of it irritates her. He has jockish Italian looks and he is as different from her ex as a man could be. That's all it is.

She splashes cold water on her face and rubs it dry with a coarse paper towel. Fingers through her hair, palms pressed against her eyes, out the door, down the hall, past the security guard who spends his days absently roaming the clinic halls.

Weasel is already walking towards her when she calls his name. He is carrying a rose. "I brought you this. Because of your divorce and all."

Ruthie takes the rose, a miniature pink bud that is wrapped in a plastic cone and that sells for $2.99 at a convenience store. She tries desperately to remember if she was indiscrete enough to tell Weasel about her court date this morning. Apparently she was. Her cheeks burn and she hurries back down the hall, hoping none of her colleagues will see them. As they pass the security guard, he notices the rose and winks at Weasel.

In her office, Weasel is restless. He crosses and uncrosses his legs, clears his throat, stands up and walks towards the window. He starts to light up a cigarette and then remembers where he is and shoves the pack back into his pocket. It's been a week since Lonny found him and there's been no call to cancel their weekly dinner at their mother's, no call to scream at him. Nothing at all.

"How did your interview at the gym go last week?" Ruthie asks finally.

Weasel reaches into his back pocket and produces a wallet that still has a barcode sticker affixed to it. He makes a show of scanning its contents but from across the room Ruthie can see how close to empty it is. He steps towards her and hands her a business card. *Robert Candor, Fitness Instructor.*

"I'm teaching there on Mondays and Wednesdays. They make me wear fatigues and act like the class is Boot Camp. But it's all right."

Ruthie cannot help it. She smiles.

"You should come sometime. It's at 6 AM. But there's a day-care."

"This is great news, Robbie."

He shrugs and, she is surprised to see, blushes.

"You must feel good about this."

"My mother is going to loan me some money to start my own gym."

"That's a big step." Ruthie's tone is neutral.

"For her or me?"

"Both."

"I want to do it my way. None of this gimmicky shit. That's not what boxing is about."

"What *is* boxing about?" she asks.

This is what pisses him off about therapy, even with Ruthie. Nothing can ever be simple. They always want to know why you do things, how it makes you feel. Really, Ruthie thinks boxing is savage. She doesn't want to hear about how right it feels to land a perfect punch. Just like she doesn't really want to hear about how good the shit he'll do tonight will feel, or about how Lonny found him, or about how he took a copy of his mother's bank statement from her apartment. And so, he turns back towards the window, knowing that if he stays quiet for long enough, she'll change the subject. The sun has already set and the buildings surrounding them are dark except for the odd security light.

But the silence does not last. A deep rumbling sound fills the room and when Weasel pivots, he sees that the battered black filing cabinet next to Ruthie's desk is crashing to the floor. He can't get there quickly enough to catch it. It lands on her foot and she howls in pain.

She tries to yank her foot loose. But it's pinned. With an exaggerated grunt, Weasel clean jerks the filing cabinet away from her. As it swings up, the top two drawers slide out and files full of patient records cascade to the floor. Ruthie is massaging her foot, doing everything she can to avoid another round of tears. Weasel kneels down and starts gathering the scattered papers.

"You shouldn't do that. I'll take care of it." She puts a hand on his shoulder and gently pulls him back. Through the cotton of his shirt, his skin is warm. She wants to hold onto him, but she forces herself to let go.

The clock above her desk slips from its anchor and lands face down on her desk blotter. They both realize then that the room itself is shaking. The bookshelf, full of journals and clinical manuals, is next to go. Weasel tries to stand up, but as he does the floor swells with another rolling wave and he falls back down, landing at Ruthie's feet. He's humiliated and he frantically tries to push himself into a squat. But before he can regain his balance, another tremor ripples across the floor and he's back down.

And in this second fall, it's almost as if he can see the ref leaning over him, his hand in the air, his mouth opening wide to start the count. It's almost as if he can hear the urgent sounds of Mr. Freddy and Lonny's yelling at him from the corner, "Get up, kid. Get up." As if he can feel the same unspeakable relief that overcame him when he chose to stay down, to lose the fight. It was finally over—the relentless training sessions, the constant pressure to buoy himself and his brother by chasing a dream he'd always known was beyond him. Over.

Ruthie slips from her chair onto the floor and puts her arms around Weasel's shoulders, letting them slide down until she is embracing him from behind. She can feel the racing thump of his heart, the sweat breaking through his shirt.

This close to her, Weasel holds his breath and tries to keep his body very still. He thinks to himself, this is even better than the Saturday-morning Ruthie. *This* is the Emergency Ruthie. He takes a shallow breath and stares at her small, capable hands, studying the smooth, vacant scar that bonnets the stump of her missing fingertip.

The lights in her office flicker and then it's dark. From the hallway, the shrill, bleating alarm system kicks in. A tectonic slide sends a shiver through the entire building and they feel it— the very second it happens—as all ten stories start to sway. They sit there on the floor of her office, crouching in the dark, made small and almost identical—just bones, muscle and heart—by this emergency, all uncertainties in their lives reduced to one as-yet-unanswerable question. They sit, unsure still whether this will pass and the differentiating tick-tock of daily life will soon resume, or whether *this* is how they will go, and only later, as ghosts, will they remember this night and say, *at least we were not alone.*

Miles from them, Lonny pulls himself out from under a rattling sink in a Berkeley Hills mansion and jams the buttons on his cell phone as he tries again to get through to Lisa's school, where she's at basketball practice. But the phones there are already dead, and Lisa and her coaches and teammates are rushing from the gym to execute the earthquake drill they've practiced so many times before, and blocks from them, Susan steadies her hand to finish pushing a dose of morphine into the veins of a boy dying from a brain tumor and then holds his hand, and in the even greater distance, Weasel's mother and Ms. Ella crawl out of the pool at their complex as chlorine waves crash over their thin bodies. Cities shake and the Pacific quivers and there is nothing to do but wait. They all know better than to fight it.

AMERICAN MARTYR

It was his mother's best friend, Janet, who finally told him. Peter was in the Chronicle's newsroom when she called. He plugged his free ear with his index finger, keeping his head down to ignore his editor's periscoping scan of the room. Peter hadn't heard Janet's voice in almost fifteen years, but it all came back immediately—her horsey laugh, her syllables in a pile-up, the density of information she packed in. The short of it: his mother, whom he had not heard from since before his wedding, needed a bone marrow transplant. That she'd had two forms of cancer in the last eight years was news to him. *It's a simple procedure,* Janet said of the test that would determine if he was a match. *We've all been tested. They even did a drive at church*, she continued.

It was like getting kicked in the gut and he had to pause to catch his breath. He and his mother had been back in touch for several years. They'd talked about their jobs, the dog, Carolina basketball, the goddamned weather. But what mattered most, she'd kept at a safe distance.

Breast cancer and lymphoma? Did she grow up next to a nuclear reactor? Felix asked as he and Peter lay in bed that night.

"It was a Piggly Wiggly," Peter replied.

**

"There are still seats on your flight. I can book a ticket," Felix said two weeks later. It was Sunday morning, omelets with hot salsa and fresh guacamole, steaming coffee in the French press, cold cream. But Peter shook his head and poured a third cup of coffee. He wanted to do this alone and he knew that if he didn't, he'd be left to sift through the wreckage of their small family: a single-engine Cessna, strewn across a tobacco field.

Peter was a match, or as much of one as a child can be for a parent. He was a 4 out of a possible 8 on the scale they used. *Less than ideal,* Alex had explained, *but better than nothing.* It had been a push to clear his desk to take three days off. He'd worked all day Saturday to wrap up a profile piece on Gavin Newsom that would run in the Chronicle's Sunday magazine and a short freelance piece.

The procedure itself would happen at Duke's Cancer Center. His mom had already been admitted for a blast of aggressive chemo that would shut her immune system down to prepare her for the transplant. The extraction of his marrow would take a few hours and then the spongy yellow marrow would be pumped into his mother's blood stream. He'd recover immediately, but for her it would be grueling—the transfusion followed by an in-patient stay of several weeks, as his marrow made its way into the core of her bones.

Packing that afternoon, Peter stood in his closet and stared at the rows of button downs that Felix sorted for him by color, the jeans, the tailored suits, the loafers. Clean, simple lines and, by choice, subdued. But still, nothing he owned wouldn't stand out in Durham. He went with jeans and a few white and blue button downs. Felix drove him to the airport. They kissed at curbside check in, the engine idling, a cop blowing his whistle and impatiently motioning cars on.

**

It was already in the nineties when he landed at Raleigh-Durham the next morning. The tarmac was steaming and the sky was a dense blue streaked by cirrus clouds. The rental car, an unremarkable Chevy sedan, smelled like pine air freshener. He tuned the radio to the pop station he'd listened to growing up. Fifteen years had passed since he'd last seen his parents. He hadn't been back to North Carolina since Alex's med school graduation.

He remembered the way home, though. His parents were already at the hospital, but he drove by the house just to see it. The lawn was freshly mowed, and yellow and red tulips were blooming. In the living room window, he could see Buster, their old hound, perched on the couch. He knew the kitchen door would be unlocked, but he resisted the urge to go inside and instead drove to the Cancer Center.

There, he took the elevator to the eighth floor, riding up with two women in scarves. He braced himself. He walked past the nurses' station to a waiting room decorated in pastels, a TV on but muted. His father was reading the paper, a cup of coffee in one hand. His hair was still thick, but entirely gray now. Peter fought the impulse to turn around and leave.

"Hi," Peter said, uncertain of what to call his father.

Ronny looked up, rimless bifocals perched on the tip of his nose. "Your mother's expecting you," he said, standing half way up and pointing toward the unit's sealed double doors. "Call in on that phone and they'll buzz you in. But you have to suit up."

Peter nodded. It felt as if he was walking gingerly across a frozen pond.

He was buzzed through the first set of doors and an orderly came out and walked him through the protocol around precautions. He put on a yellow gown, slippers, a crepey blue mask and, after washing his hands with sanitizer, gloves. The orderly pushed open the second set of doors and they entered the unit. Peter was led to his mother's room, enclosed in glass. She was bald and pale, her body both thin and bloated, propped up against three pillows watching TV.

How many times had he imagined this moment and now, here it was. But it was neither ecstatic nor catastrophic. Instead, it felt strangely normal. He knocked on the door with his gloved hand and then pushed it open.

She looked up and smiled and waved him in. He took in the tray next to her, a nearly full glass of orange juice with a straw, an array of prescription bottles. "Come give me a hug," she said and when he did, she squeezed him tightly. She wore a baggy sweatshirt that matched her scarf. Through its soft fabric, he could feel her ribs and shoulder blades; the sharp edges of her catheter pressed against his chest.

Peter sat down in a chair next to her bed. His mother's feet, covered by white athletic socks, stuck out from the bottom of the blanket.

"How was your flight?" Ruth asked.

"I slept," he said. "The airport's gotten big."

"Well, we're very cosmopolitan now," she said, rolling her eyes. She took a sip of juice and then caught her breath. "I'm a little tired. Do you mind if we just sit for a few minutes?"

"Sure," he said.

"I'm sorry I can't talk much." She unmuted the TV. As a man's smooth Southern accent and mildly handsome face came to life on the screen, Peter realized she was watching *American Martyr*.

"Our religion reporter did a story about this," he said.

"It's terrible, but I can't help it. This is a rerun of the semifinal. The season finale is on Wednesday."

The show aired on the Christian Broadcasting Network. A hybrid of *American Idol* and *Amazing Race*, it was the network's first serious shot at winning a crossover audience. Each week, contestants completed challenges adapted from Biblical stories.

On an early episode, they'd been dropped off in a gated community outside Chicago and instructed to knock on doors until they found someone who would take them in for a night. As Peter and Ruth watched, the remaining three contestants— a paunchy ex-narcotics cop from Charlotte, an anorexic-looking soccer player from Liberty University, and a perky, stay-at-home mom from Orange County, California—were told about their next challenge, which involved going undercover as an inmate at a federal prison to start a ministry.

"You're all grown up," Ruth said during the next commercial break. She put a hand on his cheek. Her skin was clammy.

That's what fifteen years will do, he wanted to say. "It's good to be here," he said instead, and the words sounded like tin soldiers marching out of his mouth. But they were not untrue.

She looked him in the eye and the tenderness in her face overwhelmed him. It felt almost suffocating.

Ruth fell asleep a few minutes later, her leg twitching, her mouth open slightly. Peter kept watching as the shows' contestants were deposited at the intake centers of three federal prisons. The camera followed the cop as he walked across the yard to the edge of a pick-up basketball game. Standing there in baggy khakis, government issued glasses magnifying his dark eyes, he started preaching.

The *Chronicle's* religion reporter had spent a few days in Lynchburg, where the show was filmed. She'd come back with a box of Moon Pies, handing them out at a staff meeting. Peter had laughed along with everyone else, but it had felt hollow and vaguely cruel.

When he was in high school, the membership of the Young Life chapter had swelled until it became the school's largest club; even his high school crush, Travis Pearson, and Keisha had joined, along with most of the school's Varsity athletes. During the week before Easter, the group would set up a burnished steel coffin—on loan from a parent who owned a funeral home—in the commons area outside the cafeteria. *This is Christ's coffin*, they would explain gravely to passersby. The group's members would spend their lunch hour gathered around it, Christian rock playing on a boom box, some of the girls in tears. As tempting as it was for him and Alex to laugh, they didn't, and nor did he write a snarky op-ed for the school paper. After all, the respective objects of their obsessions, Keisha and Travis, were part of the vigil, looking uncomfortable but still standing there in their Young Life t-shirts.

He laughed out loud as he watched the members of a women's prison gang surround the stay-at-home mom on *American Martyr*. It was easier to sit there staring at the TV than to deal with the reality of his father down the hall. How tempting it was to slip back downstairs and simply meet his parents at the hospital the next morning.

In the waiting room, his father was eating a turkey sandwich. Peter sat down in a chair opposite him. Each second felt protracted. "How's she doin'?" Ronny finally asked.

"Good," Peter said, although he didn't know what he meant by this. "She fell asleep."

"She needs it. Lots of rest right now. You hungry?" Ronny gestured towards a small blue cooler at his feet.

Peter shook his head. It was close to noon, but his body was still on West Coast time. He saw his father's eyes linger appraisingly on his wedding ring.

"It's titanium," Peter said.

Ronny paused. "They make aircraft missiles out of that, you know."

"Have you been spending all day here?" Peter asked.

His father shrugged. "I'll go home to let Buster out and run some errands." Ronny wiped a spot of mustard from the corner of his mouth. "Janet comes by every day. That livens things up," he said. He opened the cooler, reaching for a Granny Smith apple and then taking a loud, crisp bite. Ronny picked the newspaper back up and Peter took out his phone and started responding to emails. The minutes ticked by.

**

Peter had booked a single at the Hampton Inn a mile from the hospital. But instead of going straight there, he drove around Durham for an hour, looping through the neighborhood where Alex's parents, at the beach that week, lived; past Duke's East campus, where frat boys sauntered by and skinny women jogged in pairs, ear buds in; past tiendas and warehouse-sized thrift shops; past a Ford lot guarded by an infantry of SUV's; through downtown, where once abandoned storefronts and an old fire station had been converted into restaurants and galleries.

Clearly, his mother had given his father an ultimatum: Behave. And behave, they all would, as if the past had never happened. He felt his gut clench as he thought about all that would remain unsaid. But he could not deny the ways in which it was good to be home after this long exile, like power restored to a dark block.

Growing up, Alex had had the good luck to fall for Keisha, who, though closeted, was at least gay. But not Peter. From thirteen to eighteen, he, along with the every cheerleader in a twenty mile radius, had lusted after Travis. Peter had requested the sports beat for the school paper so that he could interview Travis during football (quarterback) and basketball (shooting guard) seasons, developing a facility for writing about athletes.

But Peter's obsession remained unconfessed and unconsummated, except for one blow job after their *Lifetime Fitness* class Senior year, during which Travis had grabbed his hair and whispered his name in such an urgent way that Peter felt like he was hearing it for the very first time. After being All-American at Clemson, Travis had gone on to play for two seasons as a second string quarterback for the Jets. Then he'd blown out his shoulder and had moved back to Durham, wife in tow, for law school. Now, Keisha had reported, he was an ambulance chaser, his handsome beefy face on billboards along I-40.

College had been a little better than high school for Peter. There weren't quite ten kids in UVa's gay student group— LGBTA, or something like that; the acronym was always changing—though most of their meetings devolved into rants against the patriarchy by one of the co-chairs, a lesbian who always seemed to be organizing another panel on polyamory. Peter had had a brief affair with a married journalism professor who'd gotten him a summer internship at *The Washington Post*. On a fairly regular basis, he'd slept with a football player, a running back capable of surprising tenderness. This boy was from Asheville and he'd invited Peter home with him one weekend. They'd eaten dinner at his grandmother's and gone to church with his extended family, Peter's white skin provoking stares from the toddlers in the congregation. *They think something's wrong with you*, the running back explained, laughing.

He'd been luckier than a lot of guys he knew, which meant he'd never been beaten up or arrested. But his mere entrance into a mini-mart or a men's room was often enough to provoke a menacing stare, the temperature in the room dropping. For Peter, it had never been an option to play it straight. It still made him laugh to remember that people had taken it seriously when he and Alex had briefly dated during high school.

After graduating, he had run to San Francisco, talking his way into an entry level job at the *Chronicle*, picking up shifts waiting tables at a restaurant on 18th to cover his student loan payments. Out there, he was adored for the very qualities that made him such an outlier in Durham. But he'd never been able to loosen its hold on him. Faded tobacco ads on the wall of a red brick warehouse. The rumble of a black freight train rolling past. Sirens piercing the night sky. The white clapboard church down the block, fire and brimstone messages on the marquee sign in the lawn. Buttery grits, sweet tea, biscuits, barbecue cooked right. March Madness. The white beaches of the Atlantic. He couldn't deprogram that stuff even if he wanted to. He cooked grits the first time he made breakfast for Felix. He went to sports bars to watch the Tarheels play.

Sometimes he imagined moving home. Keisha had done it. But for him and Felix, it would never quite add up. In San Francisco, they had good jobs, a tight circle of friends, and they could walk down most streets holding hands. They lived near Felix's sisters and saw them a few times a month. It wasn't clear what Durham had to offer beyond familiarity, charm and cheap real estate. His parents hardly talked to him and they'd never even met Felix.

For all these years, it had been easy to tell the story one way, all those memories layered and rigidly set by now, like sediment. He'd been kicked out. His father was a bigot, his mother too weak, or complicit, to protest. Alex was his family. End of story.

Then Felix came along, sitting next to him at a dinner party, shy at first, and not Peter's type in any of the obvious ways: Felix was balding, a lover of sci-fi and chess, a terrible cook and a neat freak. Even his underwear was ironed and folded. A far cry from the gym boys who Peter had always fallen for despite himself, the ones who stole glimpses of themselves in every reflective surface they passed, flexing their triceps and glowing with autonomous pleasure. But he and Felix fit. He had a quick, biting sense of humor; he had a kind heart and meant what he said; he loved earnestly, matter of factly, a good Midwestern boy; and Alex had adored him from the start. *Don't fuck this up, buddy,* she'd said to Peter, holding his hand as they walked home from a bar one night.

**

At the hotel, he set up his laptop, unpacked and worked out in the small, carpeted gym. At eleven, he called Felix to say goodnight. They talked for a few minutes, but Felix was still at the office and was interrupted by an associate's barrage of questions. "Let me call you back, babe," Felix said, but Peter fell asleep soon after they hung up.

He slept fitfully. Every hour, he woke up, repositioning his pillow, kicking the cheap hotel blanket to the floor. At six, he gave up on sleep and turned on the TV. He retrieved his glasses from the bedside table and peered groggily at CNN. As the images on the screen came into focus, he crawled to the edge of the bed, turning the volume up.

There had been a 7.9 quake along the Hayward Fault. Both bridges were out, along with power, cell phone towers and gas. He dialed Felix, but the call went straight to voicemail. The same with Alex, his editor, and six other friends. There were no messages on his voicemail.

He clicked through to MSNBC, Fox News, and then back to CNN. But the images were all the same, displaying colorful, three-dimensional graphics of what geologists had predicted a quake of this magnitude would do. No one could get into the city. CNN was running a live feed from a Sacramento station, a reporter standing on 580 and repeating the same three facts over and over. Behind her, flames and white plumes of smoke licked the night sky.

His phone finally rang. He picked it up, ready to hear Felix's voice.

"We just heard," his mother said, calling from her hospital room. "Are you ok?"

"You mean are Felix and Alex ok," he said, trying to control his voice.

"Yes," she said quietly.

Peter hesitated. "I should get off the phone. I'll be at the hospital soon." He hung up and caught his breath.

**

Hours later, he woke up from the extraction procedure woozy, his hip tender. His marrow was now being pumped intravenously into his mother, a procedure that would take several hours. This was only the start for her. What came next was waiting, a period during which her body would accept or reject his bone marrow. She'd told him that it would be like having a bad case of the flu, with vomiting, fatigue, fever, diarrhea.

They observed him for a few hours in post-op and then an orderly escorted him to the Family Waiting Room, where his father and Janet had spent the morning. Upon arriving, each family was given a beeper that would vibrate when there was an update. A team of social workers and volunteers manned the receptionist area. The room featured several sitting areas arranged around flat screen TV's, a coffee station, a bank of desktop computers, and a library of paperback mysteries and self-help books.

Janet and his father were on a couch. Janet stood up to hug him and his father looked up. "Have you heard anything yet?" Janet asked. Peter shook his head and sat down gingerly, placing his cell phone on the coffee table next to the beeper.

On the way to the hospital that morning, he'd left messages

with every contact he had at a national news outlet. A friend of his from MSNBC had called him back, but there was nothing new to report. The FAA had suspended all commercial flights into the Bay Area and his return flight, scheduled for the next morning, had been cancelled. National Guard and state police helicopters were doing flyovers and trying to determine the extent of the damage.

"You know who's here?" Janet lowered her voice. "Travis Pearson and his mother. Didn't you graduate with him, Peter? His little boy's in surgery. They found another tumor. You must have heard about this." She shook her head and paused long enough to take a sip of her Diet Coke. "You know he got married to this NFL groupie up there in Manhattan. A real operator, that one. She wanted Travis to change his name. She thought it sounded too country so she started calling him Luke. It's not even a family name. She made it up."

"He should have tried to rehab his shoulder," Ronny said. "He could've played another season. Look at Farve."

Janet continued. "Well, the doctors said he'd never be 100% again. So they came down here and she hated it. Hated it. She missed New Jersey. Who in their right mind misses New Jersey?"

Peter kept an eye on the television, where news crews were inching their way into Oakland.

"So one morning, Conner gets out of bed, he's four by then, and he can't put any weight on his right leg. They thought he'd bruised it, but turns out it was bone cancer. They get through a year of chemo and the little guy is doing ok. He looks exactly like Travis. Just when things are getting back to normal, they find another tumor. And, excuse my language, but that b-i-t-c-h up and left. You know what she told Travis, 'I'm not cut out for the cancer lifestyle.' She hasn't even been back to visit. He's raising Connor on his own."

"They went to get some fresh air a few minutes ago," she added, apparently the new authority on the Pearson family. "Oh, look, here they are." She waved at them energetically and called them over.

Peter wanted to evaporate. But instead he stood up as Travis and his mother approached. Travis was thirty pounds heavier, his thick brown hair gray at the temples.

"Travis," Peter said, extending his hand.

"Small world," Travis said, his voice deeper and his accent milder than Peter remembered. He managed a quick smile. He was unshaven and had dark circles under his eyes.

"Have you heard anything?" Travis's mother asked.

"They called down to say she's doing well," Ronny said. "No fever." He checked his watch. "But we've got another four hours."

"Time slows down in this place," Travis said.

The room bustled. An Indian family, a father and two teenage girls, walked hurriedly past, one of the girls wiping tears from her eyes, the other one on her phone.

"Well, you know where to find us." Travis' mother said, gesturing towards a couch across the room. Janet reached out and squeezed Travis's shoulder. Peter grimaced, but Travis seemed comforted by it. Not for the first time, Peter wondered if standing on the edge of stories as a reporter for all these years had made him too cautious about life's most basic gestures.

**

At five, Peter and Ronny were allowed a ten-minute visit. They donned robes, latex gloves and masks. Ruth was too groggy to talk. She looked small and exhausted. "There's my girl," Ronny said. He leaned over and kissed her on the forehead, his mask pressed against her skin. Peter wanted to touch her, but couldn't move. Ruth made eye contact with him for a second and then closed her eyes.

The nurse returned. "Ok, guys, time to go. She needs her sleep." Already Ruth had dozed off.

**

That night in his hotel room, Peter worked his way through a six-pack of Corona and a bag of potato chips. At home, he preferred wine and olives. But here, he wanted the beer he'd first gotten drunk on. He was relying upon a very specific hope: that their apartment was intact and that Felix was within it, able to get outside but choosing not to, checking his phone as frequently as Peter was, his index finger poised over the keypad, ready to speed dial him as soon as service was restored. He would be on the couch, reading a magazine by flashlight. Never mind the rubble on the streets below. Two miles away, Alex would be listening to a woman's breathing, prescribing some med, and then moving on to the next patient in the ER. These images, a chain leash on the panic lunging at him. He opened another beer and tried not to think.

**

The next morning—Wednesday—he and his father returned to the same couch in the Family Waiting Room after visiting Ruth for a few minutes. She'd had a tough night, spiking a fever and vomiting. But Dr. Patel said that was to be expected. *Graft versus host is tough*, he said. *We'll take it one day at a time*, he continued, his hands in the pockets of his long white coat, his rimless glasses slipping down his nose.

Peter sipped from this third cup of coffee and turned on CNN. Anderson Cooper was interviewing a panel of seismologists about what their predictive modeling suggested that a 7.9 quake with an epicenter in Berkeley would do. A thousand roads closed, power and gas out, liquefaction of the ground in the South of Market area.

"What the hell does that mean?" Ronny asked.

Peter shook his head and thought about the hotel where they'd had their wedding reception disappearing into molten liquid in the heart of SOMA.

Ronny checked his watch. An hour had passed. "They should let us up again soon."

Travis's mother arrived, rushing towards the reception area. The Social Worker behind the desk scanned her computer screen and Travis's mother nodded.

Ronny waved her towards the armchair next to their couch. She plopped down and caught her breath. "Travis spent the night with Conner. They can't get his fever down. I had to go to work for a few hours this morning," she said. "This was the earliest I could get over here."

"You can only be one place at a time," Ronny said.

**

That evening, Ruth was able to hold down ginger ale and a few bites of lemon jello. She had the season finale of *American Martyr* on when Peter and Ronny arrived at her room. The host announced that the show was collecting donations for earthquake recovery efforts. *The end times may be near,* he said, *but right now our brothers and sisters in California need our help.* A toll-free number scrolled across the bottom of the screen.

"Unbelievable" Peter said. His breath fogged up his glasses and his hands were sweating within the latex gloves.

"I'm rooting for the cop," Ruth said, referring to the retired narcotics detective who now ran a small storefront church in downtown Charlotte. The other finalist, the starting striker for Liberty University's soccer team, had over 10,000 followers on

Twitter. The two finalists stood still, their faces somber as wooden crosses were affixed to their backs.

Ruth shook her head. "Good Lord," she muttered. "Who would even think of that?"

"We *could* turn it off," Ronny said, his voice muffled by his mask. The yellow gown billowed out around him like a maternity dress.

"Lighten up," Ruth said and turned up the volume.

Peter laughed. She was right. The show was too bad to turn away from, as the contestants' exhaustion mounted and the coiffed host raced back and forth between them. The dollars raised for earthquake relief flashed in the bottom corner of the screen. Eventually, the soccer player got a leg cramp and fell over from the weight of the cross. The cop won. Ruth fell asleep, pleased with this result.

**

At nine, Ronny went home to feed and walk Buster. But Peter couldn't bring himself to return to his hotel room yet. He ordered a decaf and found a free table at the coffee shop in the hospital lobby.

Stepping out of the elevators, Travis spotted him. "How's your mom?" he asked, pulling out the chair next to Peter.

"Her fever's back down. How about Connor?"

"He was awake for a few hours. But they're having trouble getting his pain under control." Even under the circumstances, Peter couldn't help but admire Travis. He was wearing a gray button down, the sleeves rolled up, his forearms muscular and tan. His eyes were bloodshot, his breathe slightly bitter.

Travis glanced at Peter's hand. "So you're married?" he asked and seemed puzzled.

"Since September."

Travis nodded and poured sugar into his coffee.

"His name's Felix."

"Ok," Travis said, laughing uncomfortably. "That's a new one, but it's cool, it's all good."

Peter looked away. He didn't have the time or energy for this. A moment passed.

"So is he in San Francisco?" Travis asked, suddenly frowning.

"Yes."

"Is he ok?"

"I can't get through to him," Peter said, and suddenly he was crying. He wiped his eyes with the heel of his palm.

Travis handed him a paper napkin. "I got over the humiliation of crying publicly a few years ago," he said.

They kept talking. Soon it was nine-thirty and then ten. Travis suggested dinner at one of the restaurants a few blocks from the hospital. "I've read a few of your articles," Travis said as they walked down the street. "That piece you did on Eli Manning last year." Peter had gotten adept at writing profiles of athletes. It was a running joke with his agent—send in the fag for the big jock pieces.

TGI-Friday's was the only place within walking distance that was still serving food. They ordered burgers and drank two pitchers of beer. Travis reached across the table for the ketchup and his arm brushed Peter's hand. He didn't look up. The conversation between them was easy. Peter checked his phone compulsively. He had emails and texts from friends all over the country, but not a byte of data was coming out of San Francisco.

After dinner, they stood in the restaurant parking lot, both drunk, their faces lit by a yellow streetlight. The night air was warm. Peter could smell Travis's detergent and sweat. He imagined Travis at home, doing laundry late at night, folding Conner's small jeans and socks, SportsCenter on in the background.

"Do you want to come up for a drink?" Peter asked. He watched Travis' eyes and thought about all the years that had passed between them. He and Felix had an understanding about these things. It was no big deal, as long as they kept to a few simple rules. Never more than once with the same guy, never keep a secret, and always use a condom.

"Ah,"Travis began, and laughed, running a hand through his hair. "That's not usually my thing, you know."

But Peter also knew that Travis wanted to say yes. Desire and death always worked the same corner. Travis could fuck him, and they could lay side by side in that room, as blank as the future now seemed, sharing a cigarette, saying almost nothing at all. It would unburden them of at least one of these endless hours.

Siren on, an ambulance raced by and turned into the ER entrance. A couple tumbled out of the restaurant. "Holy shit," the guy slurred, recognizing Travis and pointing at him. He pulled out his phone, ready to snap a picture. Then he registered Peter's presence.

"Hey man," he said to Travis. "Whatever you need to do," he drawled, backing away. His girlfriend, tugged on his arm, wobbling in her spike heels, her jeans so tight they looked inked on.

Travis snapped to and Peter watched the minute adjustments kick in. Spine straightening, jaw clenching, face blank. The couple got into their car, lights on, engine revving.

"Just a drink between friends," Peter said evenly. He smiled and shrugged.

But Travis's phone rang then. He answered, his eyes suddenly alert, as if he was bracing for a hit from a 270-pound defensive end. He hung up. "Conner's asking for me," he paused. "Thanks for dinner, though. You didn't have to do that."

Peter watched him go, and then went back to his hotel room. He didn't sleep.

**

On Thursday morning, Peter stood outside the hospital entrance smoking. Taxis and cars came and went, depositing an old man on oxygen, a pregnant woman, a soldier in fatigues. His head was pounding and his hip throbbed. He watched his father approaching, coffee in hand, his hair still wet from the shower.

"Since when do you smoke?" his father asked.

"Since last night," Peter said. At three in the morning, he'd trudged over to Circle K and bought the pack of Marlboro Lights along with a bottle of Mountain Dew and a bag of Cheetos. Seventy-two hours in Durham and his regression was apparently complete; along with Travis, those had been his cravings at age seventeen.

Ronny stretched out his hand and Peter tapped a cigarette into it. He lit up and pleasure spread across his face. He exhaled slowly. "Your mother made me quit when you were a baby so I wouldn't ruin your lungs." Ronny reached into his pocket for two quarters, which he fed into the newspaper machine. He extracted a copy of the *News and Observer* from the nearly full box.

"They're in bad shape," Peter said of the Raleigh paper.

"What about your paper? Is your job safe?" Ronny asked.

"For now."

"You need a plan B."

"We'll be ok. I have steady freelance work, and Felix has more clients than he knows what to do with."

Ronny folded the newspaper under his arm. "Good." He

nodded, the way he would at a crisp three-pointer or a well-executed slant pattern deep in the red zone. Competence had always pleased him. He stepped into the revolving door and didn't look back, leaving the conversation because he was done talking. Peter finished his cigarette, jammed his hands in his pockets, and made his way to the Family Waiting Room.

Hospital time was measured by meals, coffee breaks, the chance to visit for thirty minutes every few hours, the numbing companionship of TV. CNN reported that *American Martyr* had topped the Nielsen ratings the night before.

"The public has an insatiable appetite for bullshit," Ronny grumbled. Peter looked over, surprised. His father was slouched against the couch, another coffee in hand, his hair dry now, cowlick sprouting. Peter had forgotten about this side of him—the fussy history teacher who watched sports and anything the History Channel aired about WWII, but otherwise snorted at pop culture. All these years, it had been easy to mention that his father shot deers for fun and omit the fact that he also grew climbing roses. *Don't sentimentalize him*, Peter told himself. But watching his father holding his sleeping mother's hand later that morning, he began to wonder who his enemy had been all these years.

After lunch, he spent an hour on the phone booking a flight to Sacramento. At least he'd be close to home. "What you've got to understand," a seismologist had said, "is that the Bay Area is still in a dynamic, fragile state." *And the rest of the world isn't?* he'd wanted to shout back at the TV.

Travis arrived at three, coming straight from court, still in his suit, his Carolina blue tie loosened. He swept into the room, a big, magnetic presence before he even said a word. Even the people who didn't recognize him noticed him. He chatted up the volunteers at the reception desk, all of whom he knew by name.

He'd been approached by the Durham County Democratic

Party to run for Congress, he'd told Peter over dinner. "I could never do it unless Conner was healthy," he'd said, draining a beer and pouring another one. But Peter saw in his face that he could imagine it, and that he knew damn well that golden local boy/pro athlete/single-parent dad would be an intoxicating cocktail for the voters likely to show up for a mid-term Congressional race. As Travis had talked, Peter's drunken mind had wandered. He'd seen Felix, dead in the earthquake, and then himself, a widower, moving home to manage Travis' campaign and help with Conner. He felt like an asshole, but at least it was more bearable than the other thoughts crowding his mind.

That had been last night, though. This was a new day.

Travis sat down on the couch next to Peter's father. He slapped Ronny on the back, but didn't acknowledge Peter.

"Connor ate a blueberry pancake this morning," he reported, smiling. "How's Ruth?"

"She slept for five hours. Pretty good for a night at the hospital," Ronny said. As the two men talked, Peter watched his father's face light up. What bad luck in the son lottery for a man like Ronny. With Travis, Ronny was at ease and all that stored up paternal will and love finally had somewhere to go: Ronny the willing donor and Travis—his own father gone for decades —the obvious, ideal recipient.

Travis turned in Peter's direction, but still didn't make direct eye contact with him. "Did you get a flight out?" he asked.

"I'm going back tonight," Peter said.

"That's great," Travis said blankly, scrolling through a message on his phone and tapping out a message.

**

At five, Ronny left the hospital to run errands. He and Peter shook hands. They said nothing about the days that had just passed or the ones ahead. Peter watched him walk across the hospital lobby, the bulge of his old leather wallet against his jeans pocket, the familiar slouch of his shoulders, the cowlick that made it impossible not to imagine the boy he'd once been, his skinny, urgent body swallowed by a pair of coveralls, changing the tires and oil of his wealthier classmates' gleaming Chevys and Fords at his father's garage, the grease that no amount of Lava soap would remove from his hands earning him the uninspired nickname Greaseball and, later, Greasyballs. There'd never been a question that he'd take over the garage, the battered double-wide trailer out back, and the old man's mounting gambling debts. But then Ruth came along. The joke was that she'd civilized Ronny. But they all knew it was more than that. She'd saved him. Waiting for him while he fought two tours; taking a second job so he could do his final year of college full-time; showing him, year by year, that rage and remoteness were not the only frequencies on the dial of the human heart.

Peter watched his father exit through the revolving crowd and then fade from sight. He imagined him behind the wheel of his truck, pushing a cart up and down the aisles of the grocery store, buying Bud, bacon, eggs, dog food. He could see it all so clearly. His mother gone, his father alone, coming home each day to a silence that exceeded even his own.

He took the elevator to his mom's floor to say good-bye and suited up again. She was sitting up, propped against the pillow when he walked in the room.

"How are you feeling?" he asked.

"Better than this morning," she said. "I've been watching the news," she said. Peter turned towards the TV; everywhere that he went, CNN seemed to follow him, looping through the same headlines about the quake.

"When your dad was in Vietnam, I wouldn't hear from him

for weeks at a time, and then it would just be a letter that was already outdated. On any given day, there was no way to know how he was, or even if he was alive. I'd watch the news every night and I told myself that as long as Walter Cronkite blinked at least six times a minute, your dad was ok," she snorted and shook her head. "In other words, I went crazy. But when he came home and got to hold you for the first time, all that got erased. Like it never even happened."

She paused and looked down at her hands. "We did our best by you, Peter" she said.

"I know," he said. He looked at her. The scoop neck of the hospital johnny exposed her collarbones and the tip of her Hickman catheter.

"You try your hardest, but it's not easy—"

"I know, Mom."

"Not a day has gone by that I haven't loved you. I want you to be happy, that's all." She was tired again, dragging her words through the dirt behind her. She closed her eyes.

A million things he could say in response, and almost all of them, he'd rehearsed over the years. But it had never been like this: a hospital room, her face vulnerable and aged, the damned johnny, muted footage of the earthquake on the TV.

"I'm happy," he said, thinking of the life he had left behind when he'd boarded the flight on Sunday. There was no way to know what he would return to.

He waited for her to respond, but she was already asleep. He leaned over and kissed the top of her head, her bare skin warm and smooth beneath his lips. "I love you," he said. Then he left.

**

Peter settled into a window seat. The plane was nearly empty and he had the row to himself. Not many people were interested in flying into a disaster area, unless they had a reason to. He waited until the last possible moment to turn off his phone, but still, there were no calls from San Francisco. They taxied on the runway and he pressed his forehead against the plastic window as they gained altitude, soaring above the dark green pines, the acres of red dirt plots in a new subdivision, the dark ribbon of I-40.

In six hours, he'd be in California, driving another rental car to another hotel room. Janet had pulled him aside in the hospital that morning. *You don't know what this means to them both*, she'd said. Janet saw herself as the architect of their reconciliation and, he knew, she considered it a gift to his mother. Years ago this would have bothered him, the way so much about home had. But it didn't anymore. How odd it was to take seriously the possibility that they were all trying, even when they managed to fuck up so royally.

In San Francisco, it had been necessary to reinvent himself. To tell the story of his life without talking about his family. To treat his memories of childhood—their annual beach trips to Emerald Isle, the heated mini-golf tournaments and games of Trivial Pursuit, his father manning the grill, shirtless and tan, his eyes hidden behind aviator sunglasses, his mother building a sand castle with him, searching for just the right shells to decorate it with—like archival footage of someone else's life. He hadn't known what else to do.

They reached their cruising altitude. *Drinks on the house*, the stewardess announced, aware that the few dozen people on the flight were not traveling for pleasure. He ordered a gin and tonic and then another. He thought of Felix, who had made the world new for him, who liked to sleep with his hand on Peter's heart. The thought of losing Felix obliterated him. He began to cry and, sitting alone in his row, did not wipe the tears away.

He thought of Alex, of his mother, his father, Travis, Conner, the long, forgiving back roads of Durham County. Of being twenty and walking the trails of Duke Forest with Alex the day after his dad kicked him out of the house, his cold hands stuffed in his pockets. It was Christmas afternoon and still, his parents hadn't called. The feeling he'd had that day—the certainty, really —that in order to survive, he had to get away, far, far away. *I'm your family too*, Alex had said and whether she knew it or not, those four words had made the difference on more brutally dark nights than he now cared to recall. Those words had gotten him to Felix, eventually. *I want to spend my life with you*, Felix had said the night he proposed to Peter.

The plane shot through the vast gray sky, over the rolling blue Appalachians, the deep green valleys of Tennessee, the burnt yellow corn-fed flatlands, the craggy peaks of the Rockies, the fissures and glimmering lakes of the Sierras, angling towards the very edge of the nation. They began their descent into the California night, and he pushed away the fear clogging his brain, all those dark visions of the future that had been haunting him since he'd heard the news. He completed the small, requisite tasks before him. He buckled his seat belt, returned his seat to its upright position, and braced himself for their landing. He did what was necessary, keeping his eyes locked on the seam of hope that they were all following—blindly, recklessly, gratefully—into the dark.

ACKNOWLEDGEMENTS

A very big thank you to family, friends, teachers and colleagues who've shared tremendous support over the years:

Chris Adrian, Wilton Barnhardt, Harry Beach, Heidi Beach, Martha Beach, Tony Beach, Tracy Bleeker, Meghann Burke, Ryan Burke, James Clemente, Janet Cooper Nelson, Katherine Eckstein, James Egan, Tom D'Evelyn, Claire Farel, Joey Ferrara, Zack Finch, Carter Graham, Julia Hanna, David Haynes, Kris Hermanns, Lori Horvitz, C.J. Hribal, Vanessa Jacobsohn, Robert Lasner, Vyvyane Loh, Kerry Maloney, Steve Mitchel, Cindy Phoel, Susan Ramer, Steven Schwartz, Peter Turchi, Kathryn Watson, Lara Wilson, Tracy Winn, and Jason Zengerle. I'm also grateful to the National Endowment for the Arts for a fellowship that enabled me to complete these stories.